Grimey Ways 2

Ray Vinci

Lock Down Publications and Ca$h Presents

Grimey Ways 2

A Novel by *Ray Vinci*

Ray Vinci

Lock Down Publications
P.O. Box 944
Stockbridge, Ga 30281

Visit our website @
www.lockdownpublications.com

Copyright 2022 by Ray Vinci
Grimey Ways 2

First Edition July 2022
Printed in the United States of America

This is a work of fiction. Names, characters, places, and incidents either are products of the author's imagination or are used fictitiously. Any similarity to actual events or locales or persons, living or dead, is entirely coincidental.

Lock Down Publications
Like our page on Facebook: Lock Down Publications @
www.facebook.com/lockdownpublications.ldp

Book interior design by: **Shawn Walker**
Edited by: **Jill Alicea**

Stay Connected with Us!

Text **LOCKDOWN** to 22828 to stay up-to-date with new releases, sneak peaks, contests and more…
Thank you.

Submission Guideline

Submit the first three chapters of your completed manuscript to ldpsubmissions@gmail.com, subject line: Your book's title. The manuscript must be in a .doc file and sent as an attachment. Document should be in Times New Roman, double spaced and in size 12 font. Also, provide your synopsis and full contact information. If sending multiple submissions, they must each be in a separate email.

Have a story but no way to send it electronically? You can still submit to LDP/Ca$h Presents. Send in the first three chapters, written or typed, of your completed manuscript to:

LDP: Submissions Dept
Po Box 944
Stockbridge, Ga 30281

DO NOT send original manuscript. Must be a duplicate.

Provide your synopsis and a cover letter containing your full contact information.

Thanks for considering LDP and Ca$h Presents.

DEDICATION

These books are dedicated to my pops Benny Ray. I love you my nigga, always and forever. Rest In Peace. Also, to the haters who always had negative things to say instead of positive criticism.

ACKNOWLEDGEMENTS

First and foremost, I would like to thank my momma Colleen, my sisters KoKo and Nene. Y'all been by my side forever. Y'all are my rock and my motivation to make it to the top. To all my fans on Torres Unit who pushed me to publish my work when I only wanted to do it to see if I could. To my kids Heaven and Za'von, everything I do is for y'all. I love y'all with everything I got. To my lil brother BayBay who was the first person to buy my book: I wish I could've signed it for you. I love you lil bro.

To my editor, I know I got on your nerves, but trust that I'm learning a lot. Thank you for ridin'. And last but not least, Ca$h and the entire LDP family, thanks for giving me a chance at something new. Y'all are a gift to the game.

Ray Vinci

Chapter One

It had been a couple of weeks since Kilo had robbed Correy for all his dope and money, but with the help of Philly, he was right back where he left off. He knew it would be hard to get back at Kilo because he was street product, so he played his cards right and waited. Correy had been recruiting niggas left and right because at the end of it all, it would be a war.

He had just finished counting the stacks of money stacked neatly on the living room table when Quick walked in. Quick was really the only nigga that he trusted, so he kept him by his side.

"What's up wit' it, homie?" said Correy while giving him dap.

"You know, getting to the money and hoping that I run across one of them Squad Up niggas." He lit up a Sweet.

"Speaking of money, I need yo' help to cop something real nice this time."

"I got you, but we need to go check on the trap in Skyline."

"Why, what's up? Everything good?" Correy asked.

"Naw. Somebody hit our shit, and I'm thinking it's one of them niggas," said Quick.

The thought of being robbed by one of Kilo's niggas ran him hot. He promised himself that he would kill any and everyone involved with the nigga. He put his money in his safe, grabbed his .357, and jumped in Quick's car.

Quick turnt up the Meek Mille that was in his deck and drove towards the east side. Correy had fallen off with Kilo because of Babygurl setting up his boy Rico. He knew Kilo had something to do with it, but he also knew Kilo wouldn't turn against her.

Quick turned down the radio and snapped him out of his thoughts. "I know we been busy tryna find these niggas and all, but my nigga, we need to have some fun, so later on we going out. Everything on me," Quick said as he turned into Skyline.

Correy nodded his head at what he was saying because he did need to relax. "Cool, but let's handle business first."

Quick pulled up in front of the house, where a few niggas stood outside on the porch. Correy immediately knew something wasn't right by the way everybody looked at the car as they pulled up. They both jumped out and walked straight inside as the niggas on the porch followed. Everybody that was in the house was quiet as they waited for Correy to talk.

"Somebody gon' explain what happened?" Correy asked.

"Some niggas ran up on this bitch and took everything!" Tay said. Tay was the one that ran the spot for Correy. He was Quick's cousin.

"Who was watching the cameras and the door?" asked Quick.

Two niggas stepped forward with their heads down.

"Who was it?" Quick asked again.

"We don't know. They just came like they were gon' cop, something then laid us down."

Correy started laughing because he knew how Kilo played. Kilo played for keeps and Correy knew it, which was why he had to get at him.

Quick never said anything. He just pulled out his gun and shot each of them in the head. "Next time any motherfucka runs in my shit and y'all let them get away, y'all dead! Now clean this shit up," Quick said, making sure everybody heard him.

"I'll be back later to drop some more work off," said Correy as they walked out the door. When they got to the car, Correy lit a cigarette before he said something. "I need to find this nigga or he gon' try and peel me for everything, Joe."

"Don't worry. I got a plan, but it's gon' take a li'l while to put together," said Quick. He turned his music up and peeled off to where they kept their work at.

He and Correy had been cool since the county jail and they were like brothers. He wanted to get at Kilo too, but he mainly wanted to smoke Keisha for switching sides.

The spot where they stashed all their dope and the majority of their money was off FM 78. Correy couldn't risk getting hit for everything again, so he improvised. They loaded the trunk up with brick after brick until it was full.

They drove around and dropped the bricks off to the spots that needed them. Quick told Correy that he had a plan, but he started planning one himself. Quick dropped off Correy and told him to be ready for tonight.

***

Kilo pulled up to Illy's spot, which was on the northwest side. Kilo made his whole squad move off of the east side because he didn't want anyone to get caught slipping. Kilo had needed to meet with everybody so he could let them know what their next move would be.

When he walked inside, everybody was waiting on him, including some of the niggas that still ran the few traps he had. Before Kilo and his squad started selling dope, they were jacking niggas left and right. That money was good, but dope money was way better. Now that Correy was out of the picture, they had no source of getting the work, so Mr. Lee hollered at his old connect.

"Alright, y'all, we been out of commission for a few weeks, but shit about to start picking back up. Mr. Lee talked to his old connect and even though it took a little convincing, he broke. Now for the amount we getting, we gon' need some of Correy's spots to move this shit," explained Kilo.

"Shit, that ain't no problem. Some of the li'l homies already hit one of his spots," said Illy.

"The nigga been hiding, on some scary shit! Why don't we make our own spot?" Felony asked.

"We gon' do that too, but I need that nigga Correy out of my way," Kilo shot back. "As a matter of fact, I got a lick for tomorrow, so y'all be ready.

Even though the squad had been laying low, Kilo had been scoping out licks to hit whenever they needed them. Kilo was about to say something else until his phone rang. He looked and saw that it was Mr. Lee and he answered it.

"What's up wit' it, gangsta? Talk to me."

"I just hollered at the connect and everything is a go, so this calls for a celebration," said Mr. Lee.

"Alright, we'll meet at Joe's later on tonight," he said and then hung up. "Look, Mr. Lee just sealed the deal. Tonight we celebrate and tomorrow we get to work."

Kilo left the house with Illy right behind him.

"Look, I'ma need your help with this money because this a lot of work," he told Illy.

"I got you."

Illy got in the car with Kilo and they drove towards his house. They had a few hours to get ready so they drove around checking out their different spots until they made it to his house. They kicked it at his spot until it was time for them to hit the club.

When they pulled up, the club was already jumping. He was gon' wait for his squad, but decided to just go in. He bought out V.I.P at the door and told them to let his squad in, then he made his way to the back of the club.

Kilo and Illy sat in VIP waiting on their squad while scoping everything out. It was a habit for Kilo to look for the next lick to hit. He was looking around when he spotted one of Correy's boys coming from the restroom. He quickly got to looking for Correy or Quick, then tapped Illy.

"Damn, nigga, what the fuck you tapping on me like that for?" Illy yelled over the music.

"I just saw one of Correy's boys, so be on point."

Before Illy could say something back to him, he spotted Babygurl and the rest of his squad come through the door. Kilo felt at ease at the sight of his squad and waved them over to where he was. Keisha and Babygurl were the first to come through VIP and sat next to Kilo. The rest gave each other dap and opened up Ciroc bottles while Kilo pulled Slugga to the side.

"Look, homie, I just spotted one of Correy's boys, so I know the nigga somewhere in here. Keep yo' eyes open," said Kilo.

"Cool," was all Slugga said and then he joined the squad.

Everything was going good until Kilo and Babygurl went outside to smoke a cigarette. They were at his car and posted up when Kilo saw someone move in on him. Kilo didn't have his gun on him, so his first reaction was to swing an uppercut since the nigga was low. He missed him and the nigga scooped him up and then slammed him hard to the ground. He heard Babygurl get slapped as the nigga got off of him. All he saw was the barrel of a gun staring him right in his face. When he looked into the nigga's face, he was expecting to see Correy or Quick, but didn't. As he was about to call Babygurl's name, brains and blood splattered all over his face. Kilo got up quickly as Felony shot the nigga that had Babygurl on the ground. They looked at the entrance and spotted more niggas running their way. At the sight of Quick, Keisha pulled her gun out and started shooting his way.

Whoever was in the way of the gunfire fell victim as the squad joined in on the gun action. They filled the street with gun smoke and shell casings as they dropped body after body. Without saying anything, Kilo jumped in his car and Illy followed, then they peeled out. He looked in his rearview mirror and saw his squad behind him. He also saw the police that had just stopped in front of the club.

Chapter Two

Lexi, Lovey, and Lisa sat in the food court at River Center Mall to have lunch so they could catch up. They were three of the baddest bitches in there and all eyes was on them. Since Kilo and Correy were beefing, Lovey hadn't been able to kick it with her sisters. They caught up on the last few weeks as Lisa and Lovey played with their niece.

"Lovey, have you ever thought about doing yo' own thing?" asked Lexi.

"Hell no! Correy would kill me! Why you ask some shit like that?"

She thought about it for a minute then answered. "I just see Kilo doing it and it looks easy. Maybe if we do it, we can do it on the low."

Lisa looked at them both and they all started laughing. Lexi was serious because she was tired of not doing anything and wanted to make money on her own.

Her thoughts were interrupted by her phone. She looked at it and didn't recognize the number, but still picked it up. "Hello?" she said through the phone.

"What's up, half-breed, where ya at?" said Kilo.

"I'm at the mall with my sisters. Why?"

"You need to be careful around Lovey, and you bet' not let her know where we stay at."

"I know. But this shit that you and that nigga Correy got going on needs to stop because me and my sisters are not gon' be between y'all's shit!" she yelled through the phone.

"Look, just be careful and watch yo' mouth!" he yelled back and then hung up the phone.

She was pissed off at how Kilo just handled her, which was one of the reasons why she wanted to make her own cash flow. She got up, grabbed her baby, and then walked out to her car.

Lovey and Lisa followed her, but didn't ask her what happened because they had heard the whole conversation. She and Kilo had not been seeing eye to eye lately and she didn't like it. She got in her car, lit up the Sweet she had in the ashtray, then pulled off. She was so pissed off that she never noticed the car that was following her.

"You okay, sis?" Lisa asked.

"I'm good."

"Fuck all that. You going to my house and we gon' chill!" Lovey said from the backseat.

Lexi said nothing as she jumped on I-35 and headed straight to the northeast side. She knew if Kilo found out about her being over here, he would be pissed off.

When they pulled up, Springhill was alive and moving. She was kind of glad that she came because she was tired of being cooped up in the house. Correy's truck was parked in front of the apartment and Lexi's body tensed up.

Lovey caught it and said something. "Girl, you need to chill. It ain't got shit to do with you. He wants Kilo," she said.

They got out and went inside and she could tell both Lexi and Lisa were nervous. She sat down, pulled out her bag of weed and cigars, then started rolling blunt after blunt. She lit one and then passed it around.

Lexi had just gotten comfortable when Correy and Quick came from the back. When he noticed Lexi and Lisa sitting in his living room, his blood started boiling along with Quick's. Quick was about to say something, but Correy gave him the eye not to. He lit a Sweet of his own and then sat at the kitchen table. He stared at them for at least five minutes before saying something.

"What's good, Lexi? You don't know nobody or what?" Correy asked while blowing out smoke.

"What's up, Correy, you alright?" she shot back while looking at him, trying to figure him out.

"You know, just holdin' down mines, tryna make sure I keep all snakes out my grass, that's all."

Lexi felt the slug he shot her way and he knew it. He was gon' keep shooting at her, but decided to let it go when he saw the way Lovey looked at him.

"I'ma holla at you later, Low-key," he said as he got up to leave.

"Make sure you tell yo' boy Kilo that shit ain't sweet and to keep his eye open," Quick made sure he said before he closed the door.

***

Babygurl and Keisha's spot in Brackenridge Apartments off Broadway was jumping and they intended on getting every dime that came through it. They both sat on the front porch and served dopefiend after dopefiend while everybody watched. They had found out about these apartments while hitting a lick on a nigga that was doing too much stunting. Babygurl and Keisha were a deadly comb because both were gangstas, hustlers, and bad as hell. If you saw them, you wouldn't think nothing of them until you crossed one.

"Damn, girl, this bitch jumping like a muthafucka today," said Keisha as she counted her stack of money.

"I know. A bitch might be out here all day," said Babygurl.

Brackenridge Apartments was behind Fort Sam Army base, which was ducked off to most niggas so the law wasn't too much over there.

"It's a lot of money out here and a lot more spots we can post up at," said Keisha.

"Don't worry, we gon' lock this bitch down——"

She had stopped in mid-sentence when she looked across the way and spotted a female looking their way. She was gon' let

Keisha know about it, but decided to let her expose herself. Once Babygurl peeped out ole girl. She started checking out every angle of the apartments. She spotted a group of niggas circled up looking their way. This time she put Keisha on game. Even though they both were dressed to impress, they both were strapped. She was gon' call Kilo, but wanted to handle it on her own.

"As soon as it looks like they want to trip, don't hesitate to let 'em have it," Babygurl told Keisha.

Keisha already had her hand on her heat when two of them started walking their way. Her eyes moved back and forth quickly from ole girl to the two niggas. The more she did that, the more she wanted to shoot.

The niggas had finally gotten to them. Babygurl was about to say something until one of them spoke first.

"What's up, li'l momma? I ain't never seen y'all around here before," he said to Babygurl.

"That's because we new to the hood," she said back, not taking her eye off of both of them.

"I see y'all getting y'all paper up out here," the other one said while eyeing both their pockets.

"Yeah, and we tryna keep doin' that, if y'all don't mind," said Keisha. She could tell what she said pissed them off because their handsome faces turn ugly real quick.

"Look here, li'l momma!" the first one said to Keisha "Y'all steppin' on toes around this bitch, so it's either you leave, or we gots something to make y'all leave!"

Babygurl busted out laughing because even with their squad chains on that Kilo brought them, they still didn't know who they were fucking with.

"Look here, 'li'l daddy'," she said sarcastically. "I'm not going nowhere. Y'all gots to bounce."

Before she could finish her sentence, he reached back and slapped her in the mouth. It happened so quickly that she didn't even realize she was on the ground. Keisha couldn't react fast enough because the girl that Babygurl was watching already had a knife to his throat.

"You need to move around before shit gets ugly," she said through clenched teeth, then let him go.

They both took off running as Keisha and ole girl helped Babygurl up.

"Thank you," said Babygurl.

"You're welcome. I'm Cassy."

"I'm Babygurl, and this is my homegirl Keisha."

She and Keisha gave each other a head nod, then she gave her attention back to Babygurl. Babygurl looked her up and down and liked how she looked and carried herself. Cassy was caramel with dark brown eyes and full lips. Her hair was straight and in a bob right below her ears. She was 5' even and weighed 110 pounds. She had a plump booty and a nice set of titties. Cassy was dressed in some purple spandex pants, a black halter top, and some purple Chucks. By the way she looked she didn't look dangerous, but Babygurl saw in her eyes that she was hungry.

"Why you tucked up in them stairs like that?" asked Babygurl.

"Shit, I saw y'all making all that money and was gon' try and get y'all for it, until they came trippin'."

"Well, I'm glad you didn't, because you wouldn't have gotten away with it," Keisha said while pulling out her strap.

"Whoa! Mama, I'm on your side."

Babygurl liked her style, plus they needed another bitch on their team. "Look, I can use you if you tryna make some real paper," she said while giving her the rundown of what the squad did.

She listened and nodded her head at what she was hearing. "Cool. I got a spot around the way if y'all want to set up shop. Look, I ain't got shit to my name, but if y'all for real, I'm down," Cassy said.

"Alright. You can meet the squad tonight."

They chopped it up for a li'l bit and were about to go when those same niggas came back with a few females.

"Bitch, y'all got a problem with my people!" one girl yelled out before they got there. By the way she was dressed, she could tell the bitch wanted to fight.

"Who the fuck you talking to like that? 'Cause ain't shit soft this way!" Babygurl shot back.

She handed her gun to Keisha without them seeing as she got ready to fight. The one that was talking shit ran up on her and hit her with a flurry of quick punches, which made Babygurl stumble a bit. She caught her balance, then went to work on her face. For her to be Mexican and short, Babygurl fought like a champ due to Kilo teaching her.

Before they knew it, Babygurl had her on the ground and was pounding her face as hard as she could. One of the other girls tried to jump in, but was cut off by Cassy as she stepped up and stabbed her in the neck. All hell had broken loose when they saw blood, so the niggas and females rushed them.

Keisha quickly shot in the air so they could back up and let Babygurl get up. As soon as she got up, Keisha handed her her gun. She did that just in time because bullets started flying their way with the quickness. All three of them took off running until they were hidden behind a building.

"Okay, Cassy, you stay here and me and Keisha gon' get them up off of us," said Babygurl.

Cassy nodded her head without saying anything and Babygurl knew she was nervous. She moved from behind the wall and

20

started shooting at whoever was standing. She was on point because when she came from around the wall, somebody was coming their way. She shot him in his chest a couple of times before he dropped dead. Keisha was right behind her, but was caught off guard as one of the girls blindsided her, knocking her gun away. Keisha was getting punched in the face when blood splattered her face.

She looked up and saw that Cassy had slit her throat.

"Come on. We need to leave," said Cassy as she helped her up.

Babygurl's gun was empty, which made her make her way to Keisha and Cassy.

They made their way to her car and then peeled off. Babygurl had made a promise to come back and take what was hers.

Chapter Three

The squad was at Slugga's house in Camelot II, waiting on Baby-gurl and Keisha. Kilo had set the lick up with them running point so they couldn't leave without them. They were starting to give up when Babygurl, Keisha, and Cassy came through the door. Everybody stared their way because they hadn't seen Babygurl and Keisha in a couple of days and now they showed up with a girl they didn't know.

"Let me holla at ya outside," Kilo said to Babygurl.

They both walked outside and stood on the porch.

"Who is li'l momma?"

"I ran across a li'l situation a couple of hours ago and she helped me out," she explained. "We was getting money and she was scheming on us when some niggas started tripping. The nigga slapped me and there she was with a knife to the nigga's throat."

She explained the whole situation to him and he wanted to talk to her himself. He sent Babygurl in and told her to send Cassy out. Cassy came out and Kilo liked what he saw: a small, sexy, but deadly young woman.

"What's up, li'l momma? What's ya name?" he asked.

"Cassy. And yours must be Kilo."

"Yeah. I appreciate what you did for Babygurl. She told me your situation and we can use some help tonight on this lick. You down?"

"Hell yeah!"

"I'm guessing you can't go back to yo' spot, so you can stay at my trap in The Landings. We gon' send y'all back with somebody so y'all three can take over those apartments. Come on so you can meet the squad."

They both walked back in and he introduced her to everybody. Kilo explained to the squad her situation and they welcomed her with open arms.

"Alright, let's get to work," said Kilo. "I been scoping out these niggas on the east side and it looks like they getting some cash. The thing is, it's two spots. One's an after hour and one's a trap right next door."

"Me, Illy, Kilo, and Low-key can hit the trap while Babygurl, Keisha, and Felony gon' hit the after hour. Mr. Lee, you our getaway driver and Cassy, you're gonna be theirs," said Slugga. That was a slight change in plans. Before Cassy showed up, Felony was going to handle the duties she had just been assigned.

"Ain't nobody gon' be at the after hour spot but the two niggas watching the door. I know y'all can handle that," Kilo said to Keisha and Babygurl as they gave each other high fives. "Here. You might need this." He gave Cassy a gun and she tucked it in her blue jeans.

They finished explaining everything and then loaded up and headed towards the east side. Illy and Slugga were up front while Kilo and Low-Key rode in the back. They loaded up their guns while listening to J-Dawg's "Everybody Lookin' Like a Lick".

Kilo had been plotting this lick for a while so he knew the payout would be big.

Slugga had exited at New Brauntels and rode all the way down to Denver Road. He looked back to make sure Cassy was behind them. They were three houses down when Kilo told him to pull over and park on a side street.

"Nobody in that house lives tonight, so do what y'all got to do to survive," said Kilo.

They all got out and made their way to the trap house. A couple of niggas were in front smoking, which threw shit off a li'l bit, but Kilo was quick on his feet.

"Say, gangsta, that shit smell like some heat. How much you wanna sell?" Kilo asked because he knew he would brag.

"Shit, whatever y'all wanna buy! Come in!"

They walked up to the trap and Illy didn't waste time. He pulled out his gun and slapped the nigga that was closest to him.

"Y'all can give us everything y'all got in this bitch."

The rest of the squad was on point as they pulled their guns on the other two.

"If any of you niggas scream, you'll die before you have to," said Slugga. "Y'all walk in this bitch slow, and if one of y'all makes a sudden move, that's ya ass."

Kilo knew it was only them because the other two were getting ready for the after hour. The trap had bricks stacked on the table, which made Kilo smile

"Low-key, bag that shit up. Illy, go check the rooms for anything worth taking," said Kilo while holding both his guns on the men.

As soon as Illy turned to walk off, one of them tried to move on him. Kilo shot once and blew the brains out the front of his head.

"Anybody else feel like dying? Let me know and I promise I can make it happen."

Kilo stopped talking when he heard shots come from the back. Slugga rushed to the back and saw Illy standing over a nigga with holes in his chest.

"Help me get this money," said Illy.

Slugga looked on the bed and saw stacks of money spread all over. He grabbed the sheet and wrapped it up, then swung it over his shoulders as Illy grabbed the few pounds of weed next to it. They headed back up front and Kilo and Low-key were waiting on them. Kilo pulled his trigga and smoked the last two niggas that were left.

***

Babygurl and Keisha had walked up to the after hour spot once they saw Kilo and the squad come out. Felony stayed back with Cassy until he saw them walk in. Babygurl and Keisha walked up to the door and it opened like they were waiting for them.

"Y'all kind of early," a big bald-headed nigga said.

"Oh, I thought y'all was starting early. I guess we can come back," said Babygurl as they turned around and started walking off. She knew once he got a look at their asses, he wouldn't be able to resist them.

"Look, li'l mama, we about to open. How about y'all come in and chill?"

Before they walked in, Babygurl turned around and looked at Felony, giving him the go signal.

When they got in, they spotted they spotted the other nigga sitting at the bar counting money. Keisha wasted no time and walked straight to him. Babygurl was glad that they didn't get searched because she had the only gun until Felony came with Keisha's.

"Why y'all let us in and y'all ain't even open yet?" Babygurl asked, making conversation.

"How could I turn two sexy-ass women down? Plus we could use the company," he said, walking up to her.

On any other occasion she would have gave him the time because the nigga was fine as hell. She looked over at Keisha and she had his full attention. Babygurl and Keisha could make any nigga lose track and slip up on his game. Before Babygurl knew it, Keisha was helping the nigga count the money. She walked towards her and Keisha gave a slight smile. Even though Babygurl was talking, she kept eyeing the money and was liking what she saw. She knew that the spot opened in an hour and people would be coming. She was about to back out until she heard a knock on the door. Both of the niggas looked at each other with confused looks on their faces.

The nigga counting the money pulled out a Mossberg pump as the other one went to the door. He look through the peep hole and shook his head. He opened the door and looked Felony up and down.

"We ain't open yet, homie. Come back in an hour," he said.

"My bad, but I didn't come to kick it," Felony said, pulling out his strap.

"What you plan on doing with that?"

When he asked that, it pissed Felony off and he shot him in both kneecaps. He fell instantly, and Felony stepped over him so he could get to the other one. As soon as Felony stepped through the door the nigga that was counting the money let the Mossberg pump go. Felony dove out of the way as the buck shots flew his way. Babygurl pulled her strap out and let him have it. The only reason he didn't get hit was because Keisha was next to him. Keisha ran towards Felony so she could get her strap, but was pulled down.

Felony quickly got up and started her way, but was grabbed by the nigga he had shot. He aimed his gun at his face and shot him twice. When he made it to Keisha, Babygurl meet him there.

"He's got her back there!" said Babygurl.

Felony said nothing as he stood on top of the bar and shot the nigga in the head. Keisha jumped up and hugged Felony, then went for the stack of cash.

They had found some trash bags and started dumping the money. Once they were done, they ran back to the car full speed, and Cassy smashed off right behind Mr. Lee.

Ray Vinci

Chapter Four

Correy, Quick, Tre, and two other soldias were on their way to the Second Baptist apartments on the Eastside. Quick had gotten the scoop on one of Illy's traps from a female he used to fuck with back in the day. Word on the streets was that the Squad was taking over and Correy couldn't let it happen. It pissed him off to hear about Kilo making big moves without him.

"Damn, gangsta, you can't be thinking that damn hard!" Quick said with irritation in his voice.

"My bad, Joe, what's up?" Correy said, snapping back.

"Look, when we get there, I want to scope the spot out."

"Why?"

"So we know what we gettin' into. Plus, maybe we can step on his toes a li'l bit"

"Fuck it, I haven't hit a lick in a minute," Correy said as he exited on E. Houston Street.

They turned in the first exit and Correy quickly realize that it was the only way out. He drove in and out and saw that the second exit was one way in/one way out too.

"If shit gets real, we gotta make sure we get out this bitch," said Tre.

The apartments were full of people and Correy could tell the money was good, which made him want to take them over. He pulled in an empty parking spot which was damn near empty and parked. He turned up the Lil Durk that was in the deck, then jumped out and posted up on the car. His eyes were on them, especially the hoes, because all five of them were fly as hell from head to toe. Just like Correy expected, money started rolling their way in no time and they took turns making sale for sale.

Correy just knew he had the spot until he saw Illy, Low-key and five more other niggas watching him from one of the hallways. Quick pulled his gun out and raised it up to let Illy know it was whatever. Illy gave them a smirk as he went back inside.

"Pussy-ass nigga," Quick said and went right back to making money.

All of them were so into the money and the girls that were all on them that they never saw one of Illy's boys sneak up behind Tre.

"Illy said you chose the wrong side," he whispered in his ear, then blew his brains all over Quick.

They were caught off-guard so they didn't have time to pull out their heats. Illy came back out with the choppa and sent a flock of bullets their way. The nigga that had smoked Tre was already back in the hallway so Illy never let off of the trigga. All four of them were ducked behind the car as Illy let them have it. Correy felt at ease when Illy finally let off of the trigga.

"Nigga, you must've forgot who the fuck you was fucking with!" Illy yelled. "You just thought you could come to my spot and post up!"

"I don't give a fuck who you niggas is. Give me that bitch Babygurl and my money and I just might let y'all make it!" he yelled back.

"Bitch-ass nigga, you ain't gon' make it out this bitch!"

Correy and Quick came up at the same time and squeezed of shot after shot at Illy and his squad. They were already out of the way in no time, so the bullets just chipped the brick wall. Quick was mad about his homie Tre being killed and wanted to pay Illy back. Quick tried to move out of their way, but Low-key stopped him by sending a rain of bullets his way. Quick quickly moved back behind the car.

"My nigga, we gotta get out of this bitch," said Quick.

"As soon as they let up, we gon' burn out," Correy said.

He was mad that Kilos li'l brother got the best of him. He had liked Illy ever since he helped him, but he had to die just like the rest of them squad niggas.

The shots stopped and the four of them got in and peeled off. Correy knew the laws wouldn't be coming anytime soon, because this neighborhood was dangerous, even for the cops. So, he didn't worry about that as he look out his rearview mirror at Illy.

***

Kilo and Bianca sat in the couch and counted the money from the lick that they had hit the other night. They had come out with $20,000 apiece and a few bricks for the traps which set them straight for a while. Today he, Slugga, and Mr. Lee would be meeting with the new connect so he had collected everybody's money last night.

"Damn, baby, I'm a lawyer and I haven't seen this much money yet," said Bianca as she placed the last of the money in the duffle bag.

"I do this for us, li'l mama, so what's mines is yours."

He and Bianca had been going strong since she got him out of jail. They had a house off Ingram Road that no one knew about - not even Slugga.

Bianca moved closed to Kilo and kissed him passionately. She loved Kilo with all her heart and would do anything for him. She stuck her hand down his basketball shorts and jacked him to life. When she got him all the way hard, she pulled his shorts down to his ankles, freeing his dick.

Bianca loved the way his dick looked and when she saw it, it made her pussy juices flow. Kilo was the only black dude that she had ever been with and he knew it. She got between his legs on her knees and kissed his dick head then bopped on just the head. Since she had been with Kilo, she had learned to suck dick because she loved giving him head. She deep throated him, which made him squirm, but he couldn't go nowhere because she had her hand around the base of his dick. She used as much spit as she could while she made love to his dick with her mouth. She looked up at him with her green eyes because she knew he loved it when she did that. Kilo was about to bust in her mouth but he wanted to fuck her so he picked her up. He put her face down into the couch so all he could see was her fat ass and pussy. He was gon' fuck, but went in face first.

"Oh, fuck baby!" She moaned and moved a little because she was expecting dick. Kilo sucked, licked, and slurped on that pussy as her pussy quivered in his mouth.

"Oh, daddy, eat this pussy! I'm cumming, baby, fuck!" she screamed. He lapped up everything that leaked out of her pussy. He removed his tongue and replaced it with his dick. "AHHHH! Oh my god I love this dick fuck me!" she screamed. Kilo pounded her from the back and made her ass jiggle.

"Damn, baby, this pussy good as hell!"

The more he pumped, the wetter her pussy got. He flipped her over on her back and saw her beautiful face as he re-entered her. Her feet were touching the top of the couch and Kilo was giving her every inch of his dick. She tried to run but couldn't be

"Daddy! Shit!" was all she could say as he long stroked her.

He knew she had just cum because his dick was white. He long-stroked her a couple more times and felt himself about to cum.

"I'm cumming, baby!" he moaned as he released inside her.

He stayed inside her and kissed her on the face. They laid there in the couch silently for a little while before Bianca said something.

"Baby, I wanna chill with you today."

"I gotta handle some important business today, but I promise tonight I'll be back."

"No, I wanna ride with you and see what you do."

He thought about it for a couple of seconds before he answered. He knew his lifestyle wasn't her lifestyle, but he did want to kick it with her.

"Cool, but once you see what I do, don't judge me."

"Baby, I'll love you no matter what you do."

She kissed him and ran to go get dressed. Kilo picked up his phone and dialed Mr. Lee's number.

"What's up, Kilo? Talk to me," Mr. Lee said through the phone.

"What time we gotta meet up with ya peoples?" asked Kilo.

"Shit, in about an hour and a half."

"Okay, let me get dressed and meet me on Skinnie's block. Oh yeah, I'ma have some company with me too."

"Okay, I'll meet you there. Be careful," Mr. Lee said and then hung up.

Right when he hung up, Bianca came from the back.

"Damn, li'l mama, you lookin' good!"

"I wanna look good by your side. Plus you got the baddest white bitch in the city," she said, striking a pose.

Bianca was dressed in a black Alexander McQueen thigh high dress that showed her curvy frame. She had on some black Michael Kors heels that wrapped around her calf. Her hair was laid down her back and her neck waist and ears was dressed with Tiffany's diamonds. She looked so good that Kilo wanted to sex her down one more time before they left. He got up to shower and get dressed. When he came out, he was dressed down in Gucci from head to toe and together they both looked good.

"Look, li'l mama, today we about to meet some new connect. So to let you know, shit about to get real and we might need a good lawyer."

"Well, I am that, but what type of cash y'all talking about paying me?" she asked, playing, but being real.

Just know its gon' be a nice li'l chunk of change as long as you keep us out of jail."

"You know I will do anything for you, daddy," she said while kissing him then making her way to his truck. "Baby, why don't you let me drive today?"

"Cool, let me get some shit out of my truck."

She knew he was going to get his guns. Even though she didn't want him to have them, it made her comfortable at the moment because of what he was doing. He came back and got in the passenger seat of her B.M.W and they made their way to Shunnies block. On the way he stopped at his trap in Woodlawn and grabbed three duffle bags full of money for the work.

They had made it to Shunnies block and he spotted Slugga and Mr. Lee parked next to each other.

"What's up, gangsta? Let's do this," said Kilo.

They both looked inside and Slugga spotted Bianca.

"What's up, Bianca, how you doin'?" said Slugga.

"I'm good. Tell my cousin I said what's up," she said while smiling.

They got in their whips and pulled off and she got right behind them.

It took them twenty minutes to get to Medical Drive and Kilo was growing anxious by the minute. They pulled up and got out and Bianca stayed in.

"Why get dressed up if I can't show you off?" he said.

She smiled and got out and then wrapped her arm around his. Mr. Lee's and Slugga's eyes were glued to her as they made their way up the long driveway. When they got inside, the place was fly as hell and Bianca liked it so much. They were escorted to the den, were they met Escobar.

"Mr. Lee, long time no see. How's it goin'?" Escobar asked while shaking hands.

"I'm good. This is Kilo and Slugga. These are my li'l homies that trying make big moves."

Escobar looked at them then Bianca and liked what he saw. "And what can I do for y'all?"

"We tryna take shit over, so if the deal is good, I guarantee you won't be disappointed," Kilo said.

"I can do y'all $15,000 a piece, but the load is 30 bricks. Nothing less."

"We can do that," he said, holding out his hand to seal the deal.

They made the exchange and made their way back to Woodlawn apartments.

He was glad that the deal was done. Now he could focus on Correy and taking over.

Ray Vinci

Chapter 5

Detective Stronbone had just sat at his desk when his phone rang. It had already been a long day and he just knew once he answered it, it would be longer.

"Detective Stronbone," he said, answering his phone.

"Sorry to bother you, but the Chief wants you to check out these two homicide cases."

"Don't you have somebody else on those cases already?" he asked.

"Yeah, but he thinks Kilo might be behind one of them, if not both."

He gave a deep breath and leaned back in his chair, then gave it a quick thought. He had been wanting to put him and his squad in prison, but they always seemed to get away.

"Alright, tell him I'm on it." He hung up, then made his way out of the door.

He hustled down to the ME's office so he could find out what he could about the victim. He collected addresses and any info he could and then headed to his car. The first address on his list was in Skyline, so he started that way. When he got to Skyline, people were up and about and one house had movement left and right. He wasn't there to bust nobody for drugs, but would give somebody a hard time. For some reason, he knew that Kilo didn't have anything to do with this side of town. He got out and he noticed how everybody looked at him crazy.

"Who's the damn motherfucker that's running this shit?" he asked while holding up his badge.

Everybody on the east side knew who he was so he really didn't have to show his badge. When nobody answered, it pissed him off and made him walk up to the porch.

"Look, I don't gave a fuck about what you black bitches are selling out this bitch, but when you start killing people and only hiding them down the street I come in!" he said in their faces. "Just know that for the next few weeks, I'll be up y'all's asses knee deep until I find out what happened."

He made his point, then got back in his car and made his way to Denver Road. On the way down North Brounfels, he spotted someone he just had to pull over. He hit his lights as he got behind the car and pulled it over. When the car pulled over, he got out and walked up to the driver's side.

"Hey there, beautiful," he said.

"What do you want?" Lexi asked with frustration.

"You know I want Kilo's black ass and I'm hoping you could help me out with that. "

"You can keep trying because I'm not gon' help you with nothing. If you don't have nothing to arrest me for, I would like to leave."

"I really hate to bring you down with Kilo since that baby girl of yours gon' need somebody around," he said with a smile on his face.

"How about I file harassment charges on you?" she said as she cranked her car up.

He stepped back so she could drive off and he walked back to his car.

He got to Denver Road. The house and the after-hours spot were right next to each other. He went through the process he went through every time he was on the case. Unlike the other case, he knew Kilo and his squad had something to do with this. He wrote down some more notes and went about his business. Thoughts ran through his mind on how he would get Kilo and he knew this would be the one to put him away.

***

Kilo, Felony, and Mr. Lee had pulled up to Deerwood where Babygurl and Keisha made their money. Kilo was on alert because Correy and Quick still came through sometimes. Babygurl and Keisha stayed in the back of the apartments so Correy didn't know they were still trappin'. Part of it was because they really didn't have no work, but now shit was about to change. He got out and grabbed the duffle bag with six bricks in it.

They walked up to the door and knocked. They didn't have to wait too long because Babygurl knew they were coming. When the door opened, Cassy stood there in some short spandex shorts and a sports bra. Kilo and Mr. Lee walked in, but Felony stood there and looked Cassy up and down.

"I'ma get up with you in a li'l, bit li'l mama," said Felony as he walked in. She smiled and then walked right behind him.

"What's up, Felony?" Babygurl asked.

"I'm good. How the money looking out here?"

"I don't know, but we about to find out."

"Shit, we can make a few rounds if y'all want to," he said because he knew Correy still trapped out here.

She shook her head to let him know she could use their help with these apartments.

They all sat at the table and helped break the bricks down and bag them up. When everything was bagged up, the girls got dressed and grabbed their guns, then left.

"So what's the plan?" Babygurl asked Kilo.

"Shit, we let niggas know you in charge and if they coppin', they come to you. If niggas get to trippin', then it's the hard way," Kilo explained.

She already knew what he meant when he said the hard way, so she was ready for whatever. All six of them had made their way around the apartments, letting niggas know that they had the work for the low. Some niggas bought some on the spot and some took Babygurl's number or address. They had started making their way towards the middle when they spotted a group of niggas chilling on the steps.

"Look out. I'm finna go see what up with these niggas. It look like they gettin' a li'l cash," said Kilo.

"I'ma roll with you," said Mr. Lee.

"Naw, I'm good."

Kilo walked to them and all five of them gave him crazy looks.

"What's up, gangsta? We know you?" one of them said, standing up.

"Naw, but I'm Kilo and some of my homegirls got a trap out here, and they tryna see if y'all tryna cop something!

"Ha! Nigga, is you crazy!"

One of the other niggas must have recognized his name and pulled out his phone, then texted something. Kilo was too busy looking at the one who was talking to him crazy to notice ole boy pull out his phone.

"Look, homie, I don't want no trouble. I'm just tryna make ends meet," said Kilo, trying to calm shit down before it got out of hand.

"I know you don't, so burn off, bitch-ass nigga!"

Kilo moved so fast that he didn't know that he had got punched in the mouth. Kilo dropped him and was on him with the quickness, raining punches down on his face. His squad was over there in no time and had their burners out just in case shit got out of hand.

"You niggas betta stay still if you wanna live," Felony said with his gun pointed at them.

Mr. Lee had pulled Kilo off of the nigga and told him that was enough.

"You niggas can't post out here no more. This our spot," Kilo said and then he walked off with his squad right behind him.

He was pissed off and everybody knew it, so they didn't say nothing. He was gon' keep walking around, but wasn't in the mood, so he headed back to his whip. Before he could move it back to the apartment, bullets were flying their way.

They didn't know where they were coming from so they dove straight to the ground. They all had their guns drawn, ready for the bullets to stop coming so they could go to work. Kilo felt trapped because he knew who was behind this shit. He'd be damned if he let Correy take him out like this. He looked at Baby-gurl, who was on the side of a car, and he made his way towards her.

As soon as he got to her, the gunshots stopped and the whole squad raised up at the same time, firing at everything moving. Kilo and Babygurl were dropping niggas one by one as they moved though the building. Kilo had spotted Correy and Quick, then remembered Illy telling him about the niggas tryna get at him.

"You gon' need more than this for a gangsta like me. I live for this shit. You must've forgot who got yo' bitch-ass this spot. You ain't shit without me!" he yelled.

Correy didn't answer, but let his gun do the talking for him. Bullets chipped the brick next to Kilo's head, causing him to fall back. The rest of his squad came to where they were and let loose on Correy and whoever was standing around him. When Correy saw everybody dropping dead around him, he told Quick to come on as they turned and ran. Kilo wanted to follow them, but thought twice on it.

"Everybody good?" he asked his squad.

"Yeah, we good," Felony said.

They made their way back to Babygurl's spot. Kilo was still pissed off. Felony sat down on the couch and Cassy sat down next to him. She lit a blunt and passed it straight to him without hitting it. She got up and came back with a cup of Grey Goose and Tampico grapefruit juice.

"Damn, li'l mama, what I do to deserve this?" he asked as she sat back down next to him.

"Nothin'. I just like the way you handle yours." She was feeling Felony's thug appeal and she knew he was feeling her. She needed a nigga that could hold his own and she knew he could. "I might need you to teach me how to move like you," she said seductively.

"I'll teach you anything you need to know and move," he shot back then passed her the blunt.

"Don't start no shit, li'l daddy."

"If I do, I promise I can handle it."

"Um, I bet you can."

Babygurl had walked up on their conversation and gave them a nasty look. "Y'all nasty asses need to take that shit somewhere else," she said, then finished her sentence in Spanish

Kilo was gon' tell Babygurl to mind her business, but his phone rang. He looked at the caller ID and saw that it was his li'l bro so he picked it up.

"What's up, gangsta? Talk to me," Kilo said through the phone.

"Damn, nigga, where the fuck you at? Me and Lexi been calling you for the last past hour?" said Illy.

"I'm at Babygurl's shit. We just ran into the nigga Correy and let him have it, but the nigga got away."

"That's good. We at yo' crib with Lexi and she said Stronbone pulled her over."

"What! Put her on the phone!" Kilo said, pissed off. She must have been right there because she got right on the phone.

"I just got pulled over again because of yo' bullshit. I'm tired of getting caught up between you and those streets, Kilo.

I'm leaving to go to my sister's house and don't come to start no shit!" she said, crying through the phone.

He was so pissed off that he threw his phone up against the wall. Everybody looked at him like he was crazy because they didn't know what was going on.

"Nigga, what the fuck is wrong with you?" said Mr. Lee.

"Who the fuck this bitch think she is?" Kilo said with spit flying out of his mouth.

"Who?" Babygurl jumped in.

"Lexi got pulled over by Stronbone today because of me. The bitch got loud, talking about she going to her sister's house."

"I told that bitch I would kill her if she fucked over you."

"Naw, if I go over to that house, her shit betta be gone. Fuck that bitch. I finna go handle some business. I'ma be back to get y'all."

Kilo left without saying nothing to nobody. Babygurl knew Kilo was fucked up about Lexi and she was gon' get at her when she least expected it.

Ray Vinci

Chapter 6

Lexi had been over at Lovey's house for three days and hadn't heard anything from Kilo. She was fed up with him and his street shit and intended to let him know. She and Lovey were going to Taboos tonight to get Kilo off her mind. Even though she was mad at him, she missed him more than anything. When she had finished getting dressed, she went to the living room to kick it with Lovey.

"Now that's what I'm talkin' about! Get with the program. You can't let that nigga bring you down," Lovey said.

"I know. That's why 'Im going out tonight. Do you think Kilo will ever change?"

"Girl, you can't expect to change no nigga like Kilo. He been in the streets all his life, so you can't expect more or less. Yo' ass used to go crazy behind that nigga, and now you just let him go."

"I know, but now he has a baby and I need to think about mine."

Lovey didn't get to say anything because the door opened and Quick walked in by himself. He looked at them and walked straight to the back as their eyes followed him.

"Girl, that nigga too fine for his own good," said Lexi.

"You ain't never lied, and his sex game is on point too," Lovey shot back.

"You need to stop before Correy kill yo' ass."

Lovey said nothing as she reached in the ashtray and lit the half a Sweet. They passed it back and forth and conversed for a li'l while until Quick came back through.

Quick made Lexi nervous and she didn't know why. She knew Kilo was mad just at the thought of her being around his enemy. He stopped and looked her in her eyes, which made her more nervous. She was gon' look away, but she knew he was trying to scare her.

"Quick, you need to leave my sister alone. You leave that shit between y'all and Kilo. He respects me enough not to bring shit to my house, so you need to respect that shit too," Lovey said, checking him.

"Fuck that nigga! Ain't no love for that nigga this way. Next time I run across the nigga, he a dead man," he said with anger as he walked out the door slamming it.

"You know what? I'm just gon' leave and get a hotel. It's clear that they don't want me around," Lexi said.

"Bitch, you ain't going nowhere. If anything, they leavin', so sit yo' ass down somewhere."

Lexi loved her sister and knew she could depend on her for anything. They sat there and smoke until it was time to hit the club. They were gon' drink, but decide to hold off until they got there. When they left the house it was 9:00pm and they felt like the baddest bitches on earth.

Taboos was in the middle of downtown, so it didn't take too long to get there. When they got there it was packed, so it took them a little while to find a parking spot.

"Damn, bitch, this club is full of niggas!" said Lovey as they walked up to the line. Lovey knew the bouncer and paid him $100 to get in.

When they got in, bitches were bouncing their asses on niggas as Migos blasted through the speakers. They walked straight upstairs and went to the bar, then ordered two hurricanes.

"Bitch, I'm not finna sit here with you when I can be dancing with one of these fine-ass niggas!" Lovey yelled over the music.

"Bye, bitch, I'm not stopping you." Lexi sipped her drink.

Lovey walked to the dance floor with her drink and started popping her ass on a dark-skinned nigga. Lexi started laughing and shaking her head.

"Why sit here alone when you can be doin' the same thing?" a voice asked.

Lexi looked to her side and spotted one of the sexiest Mexicans she had ever seen. She was gon' turn him down, but the nigga was fly and she did come to have fun. She told herself fuck it as she set down her drink, grabbed his arm, and headed to the dance floor.

***

They walked in the club and all eyes was on them. Everybody knew how they rolled, so it was nothing but respect. Most bitches were scared of them and most niggas knew if they crossed any line they would lose their life. Babygurl, Keisha, and Cassy had bought out VIP just because they could. They were known because of Kilo, but Babygurl had her own plan and was slowly putting it together.

All three of them finally made it to VIP, which was full of peach Ciroc and Grey Goose. Babygurl wanted to show her homegirls a good time, so she paid for everything. Cassy stood on the couch and started dancing and Babygurl and Keisha followed suit. They were feeling the peach Ciroc they were drinking and started throwing money. Babygurl stopped dancing when she looked past the crowd and saw a familiar face.

"What's wrong with you?" Keisha asked because she knew her girl was mad all of a sudden.

"I think that's that bitch Lexi over there shaking her ass all over that nigga."

Keisha and Cassy looked across the floor and saw Lexi and Lovey on the dance floor. They both already knew what time it was with Babygurl when it came to Kilo. She was already zero tolerance with the squad, but Kilo was a different story. Kilo would always be her nigga no matter what.

"I'm about to go get my heat. The bitch gots to die tonight," said Babygurl.

"Naw, not in here, but we can beat that ass," Cassy said.

"Hell yeah!" said Keisha.

They all took off the jewelry they had on and stuffed it in their pocket. They had confidence in their hands and knew it wouldn't be a problem stomping them out. As they made their way through the crowd, it parted as if they knew something was about to go down. Babygurl was the first one to get there as she grabbed Lexi by the hair.

"I told you if you fucked over Kilo, I would beat yo' ass," she said as she hit Lexi in the face.

She had put a lot of force behind the punch because it put Lexi on her ass. She was gon' get on top of her, but wanted to see what she had and let her get up.

"I been waitin' on this," Lexi said, taking off her heels.

They posted up as the crowd formed a circle. Lexi threw two quick punches that didn't hold no weight, but pissed Babygurl off. Babygurl threw a flurry of punches at Lexi as she rushed her, connecting with every blow. Lexi covered her face as much as she could, but still felt them. She fell backwards, but this time Babygurl showed no mercy by jumping on her. Babygurl had Lexi's hair wrapped around her arm and pounded her face with the other. Lovey let them fight until she saw blood coming from Lexi's face.

Lovey was already moving in on Babygurl, but was stopped short as Keisha and Cassy went crazy on her face. Lovey could hold her own, but against two, she was useless. Lovey fell right next to Lexi and all three of them started using their feet.

They had only gotten off a few kicks before the bouncers grabbed them.

"You betta not fuck with Kilo or I'ma smoke both y'all ass," Babygurl yelled as they dragged her to the door.

"Y'all get outta here before the laws come," the bouncer said. "Tell Kilo and them I said to holla at me."

They made their way to the car and smashed off. They weren't even on the freeway good when her phone rang. She already knew it was Kilo because when it came to her, news got to him fast.

"Hello?"

"Girl, what the fuck y'all got going on in Taboos?" Kilo asked.

The car was quiet so all of them could hear him. For some reason, they all felt like they were in trouble.

"Yo' girl was in that bitch grinding on another nigga, so we beat them hoes down."

"Oh yeah? The bitch bold enough to do some shit like that?"

Babygurl knew he was mad and knew he was trying to play it cool. "That's alright, baby, I got this. Let me handle it," she said, trying to make him feel better. "I'm on my way. I got some dank and a bottle."

"Alright," he said and then hung up.

"We about to go kick it with Kilo for a li'l while."

"Cool, we ridin' with you 'cause we damn sure ain't ready to cut our night short," Cassy said, smiling.

"Look, y'all, nobody knows where Kilo stays and we want to keep it like that."

Neither one of them said nothing so she took that and rolled with it.

They made their way to Kilos house in no time because she was flying down Highway 90. Kilo heard them pull up and opened the door before they could get out. When they got out, he could tell they were close to each other by the way they acted.

"Damn, y'all lookin good. What was y'all tryna do, attract every nigga in the club?" he said and then gave them each a hug.

They all went in and Keisha and Cassy were amazed at the house. They sat up for hours smoking and drinking until Kilo called it a night. He told them they could stay if they wanted and then left.

Babygurl caught him in the hallway before he was in his room. "Kilo, let me make you feel better."

He was gon' say no, but he could never say no to his fine li'l Mexican. "Cool, come holla at me tonight."

She left and went back to her girls. "Look, I need y'all's help."

"What's up?" Keisha said.

"Kilo is fucked up and I wanna make him feel like the boss nigga that he is."

"What you got in mind?" Cassy said.

"We gon' go in his room and take his mind off that bitch."

Keisha and Cassy both looked at each other and shrugged their shoulders. They knew this was a one-time offer and had to jump on it.

"This is a one-time thing so if I find one of you bitches fucking with Kilo after this, y'all know what time it is. I'ma go in first then I'ma call y'all in."

She went back to Kilo's room. When she got in there, Kilo was laying in the middle of his big-ass bed in his boxers. She stripped down naked, then climbed on top of him.

"I got a surprise for you, daddy."

"Oh yeah? What is it?"

She didn't answer him as she kissed him passionately down his body. She had made it to his boxers and pulled them down, exposing his dick. To her, it seemed like his dick got bigger every time she saw it. She stuffed his dick in her mouth and made love to it for at least ten minutes.

She came off of it grabbed her phone and texted Keisha. Seconds later, Keisha and Cassy came in, which surprised Kilo.

"I told you I had a surprise for you. You got us all night, and you betta put it down for us."

Keisha and Cassy got naked and Kilo's dick got harder.

"Damn, Babygurl, I see why you invited us. He got enough dick for all three of us," Keisha said as she made her way to the bed. She had always wanted to fuck him, so she wasn't shy.

Cassy was right behind her and was just as eager to please him. Babygurl straddled his face and let him go to work on her pussy. Keisha took his whole dick in her mouth and Cassy put her mouth around his big balls.

Babygurl knew they had ahold of him because he lapped at her pussy fast, making her cum quick. He felt Keisha stop sucking his dick and felt her warm, wet, tight pussy around him.

"Oh shit! Damn, I can't even sit all the way down. Fuck!" she moaned as she bounced slowly up and down.

Cassy still had his balls in her mouth, which made Kilo go crazy. Babygurl got up so he could see what was going on. He saw all of Keisha's red ass bouncing on his dick.

"Umm, I'm c-cumming! Fuck, this nigga got some good dick!" Keisha said, cumming on his dick.

He moved her, got up, and picked Cassy up. He sat her on his dick, then slammed her down.

"Ahhh! Shit!" she yelled and put her face in his shoulders

She let him have his way as she enjoyed every inch of his dick game. She had never been fucked so good or had a dick as big as his, so she came multiple times. He hadn't even nutted yet and Cassy got off and got on her knees to suck his dick. Keisha was right next to her as they both attacked his dick.

Babygurl sat back and watched Kilo nut on both of their faces and in their mouth and it turned her on. She saw that his dick was still hard and knew it was her turn. She got on the bed on all fours, then stuck her fat Mexican ass in the air. Kilo got behind her on his tip toes and plowed down in her.

"Oh fuck! Daddy! Fuck me! Fuck my pussy, papi," she scream out loud and then started speaking Spanish.

Kilo loved when she talked Spanish and sped up. She ran from him because it was too much for her to take. He put her on her back and put her knees to her chest. He long stroked her and made sure she felt every bit of him.

"Yes, papi, yes! I'm cumming. Beat it up, daddy. Fuck me good with this big black dick. I miss this dick," she moaned.

"You love daddy dick, don't you? You'll do anything for daddy dick, right?

"Yesss!"

Keisha and Cassy were watching from the side and couldn't wait to get their turn again.

He pounded and pounded until he pulled out and came on her stomach. She laid him on his back and all three of them kissed, sucked, and fucked him all night.

Chapter 7

The whole squad was together at Kilos old spot where they had a couple of niggas cooking up dope. They had just got a new batch and had the streets pumping with powder and crack. They were still hitting licks which was why they were here. Felony had found out where Correy had one of his traps and was gon' take it over. Kilo, Low-Key, Slugga, Illy, Mr. Lee, and Felony was shooting dice on the porch while Babygurl, Keisha, and Cassy watched.

"Back doe li'l Joe!" Kilo yelled and the dice hit deuce-deuce. "Money, nigga!" Kilo was killing 'em as Babygurl cheered him on.

Babygurl and her li'l squad made money through the sales.

Cassy saw Felony losing, so she pulled him to the side. "Let me see your work."

"What type of shit you on?"

"I just wanna see. You got money and all these sales comin' through. Look, what I gotta do to be yo' girl?"

He smiled and nodded his head because Cassy was trying to look out for him. "You was already that and didn't know it." He handed her his work and went back to the dice game.

Everybody was so into the dice game that they never saw the white Honda pull up. Cassy raised her head and was the first one to see Lisa get out.

"Who the fuck is that bitch? She looks like one of them bitches we beat the other day," Cassy said to Babygurl on the low.

Babygurl saw Lisa get out and got angry. She pulled out her gun and pointed it her way.

"What the fuck you doing over here? I ought to smoke yo' ass just because of yo' sister's bitch ass!" Babygurl said, getting everybody's attention.

Everybody looked up and Slugga noticed that she was talking about Lisa.

"Sit down somewhere, Babygurl. What's up, baby, you good?" Slugga said as he got up and kissed her.

"Yeah, I'm good, baby. Kilo, I got Heaven in the car if you wanna see her."

Kilo jumped up and went to the car for his baby. "What's up with Lexi?" Kilo asked.

"Even though she got her ass beat, she good."

"She deserved what she got. She left me and then a couple of days later she's in the club poppin' her ass? If I was there, somebody probably would be dead."

"Look, I came by to let you know she wants me to pick up her shit!"

"I'll drop it off at ya house later on." He kissed his daughter, then handed her to Lisa. He pulled out a stack of money and peeled off $1,000, then handed it to her.

"Give her that for my li'l mama," he said.

He went inside and the squad followed him. They all sat in the living room and passed Sweet after Sweet around until it was time to go to work.

"Okay, y'all, this shit is easy, so it ain't really too much work, but it will be a lot of shooting," said Felony.

"Shit, my favorite game," Illy said, pulling out his twin 45's

"Well, it betta be all our favorite game because Correy's got that bitch locked down with niggas."

"That's because the nigga know we gon' hit his shit," Lowkey said, adding his two cents.

"Where is this spot anyways?" Kilo asked. He was blind to this, but trusted his homie on it.

"Dietrich Road. One gate is to go in and one gate is to go out, so we have to go in that bitch and kill anything that looks suspect," Felony explained.

They all nodded their heads in agreement, which made each of them feel comfortable.

"I got three nigga out there right now just in case shit gets to out of hand," he said.

"Cool, let's get this out of the way," Mr. Lee said.

They had a selection of guns on the table. Kilo grabbed a choppa with two extra clips while the rest grabbed what they could. They got in their whips then headed to Dietrich Road to take over one of Correy's spots.

***

Correy had just gotten his team of killas together and was getting ready to ride down on Kilo's trap. He didn't keep too many niggas around him because of trust issues, so he would pay niggas to ride. He had a few niggas of his own, but he needed more when it came to Kilo and his squad. He really wanted to kill that bitch Babygurl because of what she did to Lovey and Lexi.

Kilo was taking over the city slowly but surely and he had to do something about it. The Landings used to be his, but when he and Kilo started beef with each other, Kilo took over. There were ten of them altogether and they planned on taking it back. Kilo kept a team of niggas in every spot he had, so it was hard to get in.

"Okay, y'all, we goin' in this bitch ten deep and tryna leave the same way. This nigga got a bunch of hard heats that will murk anything moving, so go in with murda on ya mind," Correy explained.

None of them said anything but were ready to go in and kill. He knew Kilo wouldn't be there, but he still wanted to take it over.

The Landings was right down the street, so they got there in minutes. When they rolled in the Landings three cars deep, the niggas in front stared at them crazy so they drove straight to the back. They saw niggas posted up, but not a lot, and Correy knew there would be a lot more.

Correy sat up front and loaded up his two Glock 9's and his AR-15. Quick lit up a Sweet and they floated it back and forth.

"I want this spot," Correy said

"Well, let's go get it."

They got out and the rest followed right behind them. They all looked up to no good and intent on letting everybody know it.

Correy was stopped by one of the niggas that used to be down with him. "What up, homie? Last time I checked, y'all wasn't supposed to be around here," the nigga said to Correy.

Before Correy could respond, Quick said something. "Well, guess what? We go where we wanna go." He blew a quarter size hole in his forehead.

All hell broke loose when the gunshot went off. The niggas in the front of them were laid to rest with ease. When they looked around, niggas were bending the corner with their guns out. Correy was quick on his toes and let the AR-15 loose and smoked everyone that hit the corner.

Quick started moving forward towards the front of the apartments, but was cut off by buckshot. He was almost hit, but was saved by Correy. Correy had handled the nigga that was almost standing over his homeboy.

"You owe me one," Correy said to Quick and helped him up.

They immediately went to work, not playing games, killing every nigga that wasn't with them. Correy spotted one of his killas squatting behind a dumpster cornered, but was too late. He watched him get gunned down. Quick was dropping niggas left and right. One was shooting at Correy from the stairway and

Quick made it up there in no time. He didn't even see him coming as Quick shot him three times in the chest.

"We even!" he yelled down to Correy.

They niggas that had been at the front when they first came in were on their way to them. There were only six of them now and they all rained shots down on the ones that were coming. Correy was out of bullets in one of his 9's so his shots had to all count.

When they finished them off, they felt like it was over until Quick yelled out, "Ahhhh, fuck! I'm hit!"

Correy turned around and saw somebody hiding behind a truck. He ran full speed to him and used his last bullets to end his life.

Quick had been shot in the shoulder and was able to walk back to the whip. Before they made it back, they assured everybody that Correy was back in charge.

Ray Vinci

Chapter 8

Correy and Quick were chilling at the house counting money. They decided to lay low due to Quick being shot the other day. They had put some niggas in the Landings just in case Kilo came through tripping. He was feeling good about hurting Kilo by taking his spot. Quick lit up a Sweet and then passed it to Correy. They were waiting on Philly to drop off some work so they could load up their spots.

"I hate when this nigga be takin' all fuckin' day to come through, Joe," Correy said, pissed off.

"You know Philly gon' take his sweet-ass time."

"I need to put my foot up his sweet ass. Maybe he'll move a li'l faster."

Quick started laughing because Correy was always complaining about Philly being late. Quick stopped laughing when he heard a knock at the door.

"There he go right there, crybaby-ass nigga."

"Shut up," Correy said, slapping him upside the head.

Correy opened the door and Philly walked in like he was on time.

"Nigga, you slow as fuck. You act like I'm still coppin zones or something," Correy told Philly.

"You always crying and shit. As long as I come, you good," Philly shot back.

Quick was dying laughing because the two always argued like brothers. They made the exchange and then Philly went on about his business.

They had went to sit on the couch to play Madden '21 when Lovey, Lexi, and Lisa came in with a bunch of bags.

"Damn, what y'all do, buy the whole damn mall?" Correy said, being sarcastic.

"You nosy. Mind yo' business," Lovey said, being sarcastic back.

They went straight to the back room with their bags and stayed back there for a little while. When they came back up front, Lisa was leaving and they said their goodbyes.

"Y'all hungry or what?" Lovey asked everybody.

Correy and Quick were so into the game that they didn't answer. Lovey and Lexi went in the kitchen and went to work. They chopped it up for a while until Correy came in. Lexi went to the living room, sat down on the couch, and pulled out her bag of doe-doe. She knew Quick was staring at her, but she didn't care. She lit the Sweet, hit it a few times, and then passed it to him. He looked at her crazy because he talked to her bad the other day.

"Nigga, grab the Sweet. You know you wanna hit it," she said while laughing.

He grabbed it and hit it, then started coughing hard. "Damn! What you got me smoking on? You trying kill me?"

"It's just some good doe-doe, plus you can't hang. You just got some weak-ass lungs."

He passed it back, then looked at her and kind of felt sorry for her. "Look out, li'l mama. My bad for goin' off on you. It's just ya nigga."

"Don't trip. I can take a li'l shit talking, plus you too pretty for me to take serious," she said, laughing.

All Quick could do was give a little chuckle as he passed the Sweet back to her. They called it a truce with each other as they made small talk and smoked.

Correy came in and they didn't even notice him because they were so into their conversation. When he saw that, an idea quickly came to his mind.

"Say, Quick, let me holla at you for a minute, Joe," he said, interrupting their laughter.

Quick stood up and walked to the back room with Correy.

"What's up, gangsta? Talk to me," said Quick.

"I got a plan on how we can get them niggas."

"Shit. don't leave me in the dark."

"Why don't you get up on Lexi?" Correy asked to see if he was gon' catch on.

"For what?" he asked back.

"To get at Kilo. She the only one out of us that can get close to him. She even knows where he stays. You can even hit the pussy, plus she a bad bitch," Correy explained.

Quick thought about it for a minute and nodded his head in agreement. He also thought about what Lovey would think about it, but let it go.

"Alright, let me see what I can put together," said Quick.

"Don't move to fast or she gon' know something is up."

"I got this."

They dapped each other up on a well thought out plan, then headed back up front.

***

Felony and Cassy had just walked in Bill Miller's BBQ place downtown and sat down. They had been spending a lot of time together lately and Cassy was loving every minute of it. He was so into his conversation that he didn't even notice Detective Stronbone until he walked up on him.

"Felony, long time no see. Mind if I sit down?" he asked while sitting down before Felony could answer.

"Man, what the fuck do you want?"

"Nice BMW, jewelry, clothes, shoes, not to mention this sexy li'l hot mama you got here. Now I know you must be back in the game."

"Man, get the fuck outta here. You came in this bitch to fish. Come on now, you know me betta than that," Felony said sarcastically.

"No, I don't. I just know you know something about what went down on the Denver Heights. You got away from me once, but it won't happen again."

Cassy sat there quietly, but looked at them as they passed words.

"I don't think you'll ever catch me 'cause I don't do shit for you to get me."

"You and Kilo's black asses are on the top of my list, and when I get ahold of y'all, I'ma squeeze the life out of y'all," Detective Stronbone said as he stood up. "Y'all enjoy y'all's food, sexy mama." He walked out of the restaurant with confidence in his step.

Felony wanted to walk right up to him and kill him. but knew he couldn't.

"You okay, baby?" she asked because she noticed the look he was giving the detective.

"Yeah, I'm good. Let's get up out this bitch."

They paid for their food and left a nice-sized tip, then left. Felony went straight to the car while Cassy went to the restroom.

Before he got in the car, his phone rang. He picked it up because he knew it was one of his clientele calling. He talked for a second, then hung up and was met by a barrel to the side of his head.

"You ridin' around this bitch flossin' that jewelry and this fly-ass whip, you gotta be holdin'."

"Nigga, you got the game fucked up. Do you know who you fuckin' wit'?" Felony said, tryna buy some time.

"Nigga, I don't give a flying fuck who you is, but I do care about what's in them pockets, gangsta," he said while poking Felony in his head with the gun.

Felony started going in his pockets and coming off of his jewelry, but slowed down when he saw Cassy coming out. His banga was on the side of the door and he wanted to reach for it before Cassy got involved.

"Hurry the fuck up before I smoke yo' stupid ass," he yelled.

Cassy saw from a distance what was going on and reacted quickly. She went inside her purse, where she always kept a chrome .22 with a pink handle. She blew Felony a kiss, winked, and walked around the parked cars. She was sexy as fuck, but he knew she was deadly. He had given the nigga his jewelry and the little money he had in his pocket when Cassy walked up on him.

"Damn, li'l daddy, that's how you roll?"

She didn't even give him a chance to say anything as she emptied her whole clip in his chest. Felony looked at her as she took everything he had in his pockets. She jumped in the passenger seat, gave him everything. and smiled. He looked at her, trying to figure her out, until she spoke up.

"I just killed somebody and you just gon' sit there?" she asked him seriously.

He laughed and peeled out of Bill Miller's parking lot. They drove in silence until they got to the freeway.

"This is yours," he said, giving her everything she took from ol' boy including his money and jewelry.

"Naw, I did that for you, plus that's yo' shit."

"I know, but in the squad, you keep what you take, plus I like that you did that. Loyalty is everything to me. I owe you, li'l mama."

She looked at him and knew she had herself a ride or die nigga. She just wanted to show him she could be the same. She didn't say anything as she reached over to unzip his pants and pulled out his dick. She licked her lips at the sight of it and stuffed him in her mouth. He almost crashed once he felt the warmth of her mouth of his dick.

She got up for a second to light a blunt, gave it to him, and went back to work until they got home. He locked the doors to his BMW, rolled the windows up, cut on the AC to 100, and turned up the Trey Songz that was playing. He leaned his seat all the way back and took off all his clothes as she did the same. She climbed on top of him and kissed him from his body to his lips.

"Make sure you take care of daddy," he said.

"I got you. Just relax and let me do this." She placed his dick at her tunnel and went down in slow motion. She rode him like it was her last ride. "Oh baby, yes!" she moaned softly in his ear.

When he heard that, he started pumping in her slowly, then sped up. Her pussy was so wet that you heard every movement over the music.

"Damn!" was all he could get out as she met him thrust for thrust.

"Baby, don't stop, I'm cumming…I'm cumming!"

He picked her up and told her to get in the backseat as he followed right behind her. He kept her on all fours as she looked back at him.

"My turn now, li'l mama." He entered her in one full stroke and hit the back of her pussy.

"Oh shit!" she yelled as he pounded away.

They both were sweating even though the AC was turned all the way up. He pounded in her, making her face dig in the seat.

"Fuck Me! Ahhh! Yes! I love this dick!" she screamed.

He was turned on by how she smoked ol' boy for him and he planned on showing her. He fucked her good until they both came a few times. Then they sat in the backseat and lit up another Sweet as the smell mixed with the sex.

"That's what I'm talkin' about! I can get used to that shit," she said, breathless.

"You might as well get used to it, because it's more where that came from. Look, I appreciate what you did, so just ride with me and I got you."

She said nothing, but Felony knew it was understood and he passed the Sweet to her.

They sat there and talked until it was time to call it a night.

Ray Vinci

Chapter 9

Kilo had to meet Escobar for the third time, but he wanted to meet him by himself. He had just left Bianca's house and headed to Sea World Road. When he got on the freeway, his cell phone rang. He answered on the first ring, not caring who it was.

"Talk to me."

"Kilo, change of plans. Meet me in Corpus Christi at my beach house," Escobar said.

"Cool, but we can't be changing shit at the last minute, ya feel me?"

"Alright," he said and then hung up.

Kilo hit a U-turn and made his way to Corpus Christi. He had never left outside of San Antonio and really didn't know what to expect. He checked his twin 40 cals and put them back under his seat. He felt safe with his guns on him as he cruised down I-35. It took him an hour and a half to get to Corpus Christi and as soon as he entered, he called Escobar to get his location. Once he got to Escobar's beach house, his mouth dropped because he had never seen a house that big. He pulled up to the gate and it opened because Escobar had expected him to come.

Escobar was standing in the doorway when he pulled up. Kilo grabbed his two 40 cals, tucked them, then got out. Kilo had texted Bianca the address he would be at just in case shit didn't go right.

"Kilo, my friend, how was your drive?" he asked while puffing on his Cuban cigar.

"It was cool," he said while holding out his hand for a hand-shake.

Escobar leaned in and stole a hug, which surprised Kilo. Escobar turned and walked in and Kilo did the same, but was stopped by two guards that he had not even seen.

"What's up with this?" he asked Escobar.

"They must search you before you come in. You must understand." They patted him down and came out with both his guns.

"And you must understand that I don't go nowhere without my two bitches by my side," Kilo said seriously.

Escobar understood because he was once in his shoes so he nodded his head at his guards. They gave him his guns and let him step inside.

The inside was just as live as the outside. Escobar had beautiful women all through the house and Kilo felt like he was in heaven.

They made their way to the backyard, where lunch was set up, and Kilo understood why he said beach house. The backyard had a full view of the beach that made Kilo feel like a king. Kilo sat and ate lunch while he got to know Escobar.

"Okay, let's get down to business," Escobar said.

"I got yo' bread plus more for the next drop."

Escobar smiled in approval. "Kilo, my friend, I see you moving far along in this game and I see that you're hungry. I got one of the biggest families in the world, the Escobar Family, and I want to bring you in. It's lovely on our side and me bringing you in means I trust you," he explained to Kilo.

Kilo was caught off guard by what he just heard so he let it sink in before he responded. He started off as a jack boy and now he had the opportunity to be one of the biggest dope boys in Texas.

"I accept your offer and am glad that you chose me. I got a few people I want you to meet later on, if you don't mind," Kilo said. "Since I'm welcomed into the family, what type of business we talking about?"

"Right now I got 60 bricks headed to your spot. There's no limit to the work if your loyalty is good."

"My loyalty is always good."

"Let's celebrate."

Escobar clapped his hand once and girls came out with weed, liquor, and food.

Kilo and Escobar partied all night in celebration of new family.

***

The squad was on and nobody could tell them nothing. Tonight they had bought the bar out, plus both V.I.P. booths. Graham Central station was jam-packed with niggas and hoes, but the squad had it turned up. Mr. Lee and Slugga had a few traps on this side of town and heard the club was jumping, so they decided to check it out. Bitches were lined up to get in V.I.P. as they spotted niggas that they never saw before. The whole squad was dressed to kill, including Babygurl and her little squad. They were already turnt up, but when they played Migo's "Handsome and Wealthy", Babygurl, Keisha, and Cassy went to the dance floor to shake their asses. They had the whole club watching as they did their thang. A couple of songs passed until they finally made their way to the bar.

"Damn, bitches, I'm tired as hell. I need something to drink," Cassy said to them both.

They ordered some Long Island Iced Teas and gulped them down ASAP. Babygurl was about to get up until the bartender pulled her hand to sit her back down.

"Bitch, what's yo' problem?" she asked as she turned around.

When she turned around, she saw a beautiful half-black, half-Asian female who put a finger to her mouth. She slid her a note which she quickly read, then looked back at her. She whispered "thank you", then gave her a number to call.

"Keisha, Cassy, we got somebody that got a problem with how we took over the club!" she told them while pointing at a group of twelve full of Blacks and Mexicans.

The group was so tuned in on the squad that they didn't notice Babygurl, Keisha, and Cassy staring their way. Babygurl was fucked up at Kilo for not paying attention and would bring it to his attention later.

"Let's slide to the car and get the straps, 'cause I know they packin'," Keisha said.

They all headed out like they were going to smoke. It took no time for them to come back inside. They had two guns apiece so they could give three to the squad.

They were making their way through the crowd as six of the niggas went one way, and the other six circled around their way.

"We air these six out right now," Cassy said.

Before the six even knew what they ran into, Babygurl, Keisha, and Cassy pulled their triggas, never letting up until all six lay still with bullet holes in them. If the club wasn't going crazy because of the music, they were now that they heard the gunshots. They took off towards the squad and made it to the V.I.P. in no time. Keisha gave Illy a gun, Cassy gave Felony one, and Babygurl gave Kilo one.

When they finally noticed the other six, Kilo, Illy, and Felony popped each one off with ease. They didn't even know what was going on until the first six were dead.

"Let's get out of here!" Babygurl yelled over the music.

"What the fuck is going on?" Low-Key asked.

"We'll tell y'all later."

The squad took off towards the exit, but stopped when they saw the police coming in. They went unnoticed because the crowd was running everywhere. Babygurl just so happened to look back and spotted the beautiful bartender by the exit door.

She told everybody to follow her as she waved them to the back door. They all left through the back door, but were still cut off by the security guard. Cassy walked up to him and slit his throat with a knife none of the squad knew she had. Babygurl stopped in front of the bartender and handed her a roll of money.

"Thank you, and it's more where that came from. Call me so I can take care of you," she said then took off behind her squad.

She jumped in the truck with Kilo and they peeled off to the other side of town.

Ray Vinci

Chapter 10

Correy was on his way to meet up with Quick when he got pulled over. He didn't have anything on him and was glad that he left his gun. For some reason he was still nervous as he pulled over while looking in his rearview mirror. When he saw that it was Detective Stronbone, he cursed to himself. He rolled his window down when Detective Stronbone got to his truck.

"What's up, Detective, what can I do for you today?" he asked politely.

"First, you can cut that smart ass tone out. Second, you can answer the questions I got for your ass," Stronbone said with an attitude.

Correy smirked a little bit, but didn't let it last long because he wanted to stay free. "Shoot ya shot."

"I know you and Kilo used to be tight, and for some reason y'all just fell off. Now I got my theory. Do you want to hear it?"

Correy sat back because he wanted to hear what he had to say, plus he knew he had no choice.

"You had a best friend named Rico that was robbed and killed by Kilo and his squad, namely Babygurl. You met Kilo through y'all's girls, but didn't get cool until y'all ran into each other in the county jail. You being a drug dealer and him being a jack boy hook up and try to take over my city. Along the way you find out that they were behind Rico dying and shit changes, am I about right?"

Correy was nervous as hell as Stronbone broke down the whole story about him and Kilo. "Look, I know where you got your information, but your detective skills suck. Now if you don't mind, I would like to continue my day without you in it," Correy said, trying not to show his nervousness.

"Look here, you dumb motherfucker. You and Kilo beefing and killing everybody is getting out of control. I won't stop until

I get both of y'all black asses. And for future reference, Kilo's going to come out on top. He's street product." He laughed and then walked off.

Correy was glad to see him leave as he peeled off. Correy sat there for a minute to get his thoughts together. Maybe he was in over his head when it came to beefing with Kilo, but he couldn't let Babygurl live.

He was in his thoughts until his phone rang. He was so nervous that he jumped at the sound.

"What's up Philly?"

"Shit, you about to find out once you and Quick get this way," Philly said.

He had forgotten about picking up Quick so he could meet up with Philly.

"Okay, I'm on my way. Just give me thirty minutes."

Correy drove off in silence until he made it to where Quick was.

Quick got in and saw that he wasn't in the mood to talk, so he left it alone. They didn't know what Philly wanted to meet about, but everybody was going to be there. Philly wanted to meet on the southeast side in the Dures apartments. Correy kept looking in his rearview mirror to make sure Detective Stronbone or any other laws wasn't following him. Quick noticed it and finally spoke up.

"Nigga, what the fuck type shit you got going on?"

"Nothin. I'm good, Joe," Correy said.

"I ain't stupid, nigga. I know Kilo don't have yo' ass that nervous."

Correy looked at Quick and then ran him the whole story about Detective Stronbone, leaving nothing out.

When he was done, Quick just looked at him. "Maybe we need to lay low from the scene."

"Is you crazy? This nigga Kilo is flooding the city with dope and I damn sure ain't fixing to let that happen!" Correy yelled while pulling up to Philly's trap.

Quick said nothing. He understood his homie.

They got out and walked inside to greet Philly and the rest of their homies. As soon as Trey stepped in, Philly went straight to business.

"For some reason, we got the deal of a lifetime, but it's up to us to make it happen."

"What's the deal and what do we gotta do for it?" Correy asked.

"Shit, take over the city. It's my connect and he giving me unlimited work, plus the bread gotta be right."

"The money ain't a problem, but taking over the city is," Quick added. He had only said that because he knew Kilo already owned half of the streets. He and Correy looked at each other and shook their heads.

"I already know about Kilo and his squad being turned up right now, but we gon' turn 'em down," Philly assured them.

"That's cool, but I hope y'all know what we going up against," Correy said.

"Anyways, the plus wants to meet up and I want Correy, Tidy, and Quick to roll with me."

All three nodded their heads in agreement as Philly explained everything.

In truth, Correy needed both work and extra niggas to fight this war with Kilo.

They had wrapped up the meeting, then Correy and Quick went about their way in hopes to overcome the squad.

***

"What's up, li'l mama why don't you let me come scoop you up so we can kick it?" Quick asked.

"I don't know, you might try to kill a bitch or something."

"Damn, I thought we was good. You let me smoke some of that fine-ass weed. Now let me treat you."

Lexi thought about it for a second and decided to take him up on his offer. "Okay, I guess we can kick it for a li'l bit."

"Where you at?" he asked.

"I'm at Chacho's."

"Alright, stay right there."

Quick was glad he started pushing up on Lexi because she was bad as hell and he wanted to fuck her brains out. He also knew once Kilo found out, it would piss him off.

He jumped in his Cadillac CTS and headed to Chacho's. It took him no time to get there since he was right down the street. He spotted Lexi standing out front with her daughter, looking sexy as ever. The tan skinny jeans she had on wrapped around her thighs and ass like they were her skin. Her yellow Baby Phat top showed off her stomach and the top of her cleavage. Her tan Michael Kors heels made her look taller than she actually was. Her hair was let down in curls, which made Quick's dick jump.

"Damn," he said to himself as he pulled up to her.

Lexi put her baby in the back and then got in the front.

"So what made you wanna kick it with me?" Lexi asked him.

"I just wanted to chill. I see you looking sad and shit, so I wanted to see you smile for a change."

When he said that, she smiled from ear to ear.

"There it go. Damn, you might be pretty after all."

"Fuck you, nigga!" she said playfully, hitting him at the same time.

Quick pulled off and tried to decide what to do with her. When he couldn't think of anything, he asked her. "So what you wanna get into?"

"First off, fire that weed up you said you had. And second, I don't know, just don't get into no shit while we with you."

"I got you," he said and then handed her a Sweet.

She lit it up, then inhaled hard. She coughed so hard that spit dribbled from her mouth. Quick was laughing as he patted her back.

"You good, li'l mama?" he asked.

"I'm good, and that shit ain't funny."

"Shit! You just got some weak-ass lungs."

They passed the Sweet back and forth and talked. She put the window down as they pulled into Big Mama's soul food so the smoke could thin out. When she looked across the street at the detail shop, she saw Detective Stronbone. Her heart started beating fast. As she stepped out, she thought about Kilo and him figuring out about her being out with Quick, or him seeing it for himself. She cursed herself out for not thinking about what she was getting herself into.

They got out and headed into Big Mama's. While they ordered, Quick could tell she was nervous.

"What's up, li'l mama, why you look so nervous?"

"Nothing. I'm straight."

"Look, you ain't got to worry about shit while you with me."

Even though he assured her she was good, she still felt nervous. She knew once Kilo found out, all hell would break loose. Lexi knew Kilo was mad about her leaving, but was keeping his distance. Chilling with his enemy would bring him out.

As they walked out, her phone rang, making her jumped. She looked at her caller ID and saw that it was her sister.

"What's up, Lisa?" she asked, sounding nervous. He looked across the street for Stronbone, who was still there.

"Hello!" Lisa yelled.

"I'm here."

"What's wrong with you, bitch?"

"Nothing. I'm with Quick right now."

"Quick! Bitch, is you crazy. You gots to be tryna die!"

"We just chillin'. That's all. He wanted to smoke with me and I said yeah," Lexi explained.

"Well, you might as well smoke all you can 'cause once Kilo finds out, you dead. I might as well get ready for yo' funeral."

"Anyways, I'll call you later on."

They pulled off and Lexi looked in the rearview mirror to see if Stronbone was following them. She let out a deep breath when she didn't see him.

"He ain't following, li'l mama, so you can chill."

She lit a Newport and leaned back in her seat. "I'm glad, because his ass be getting on my nerves."

"Look, Lexi, I ain't tryna get you in trouble with yo' baby daddy or nothing——" he tried to explain, but she cut him off.

"It ain't even like that. I can kick it with whoeva I wanna kick it with. They looking out for me, that's all."

Quick didn't say anything as he kept driving. He knew he had to do what he had to do to get Lexi to trust him.

They kicked it for a little while longer before they headed back to the house. He couldn't wait until he got to fuck Lexi and find out where Kilo was. It was gon' take a while to get to Kilo and Quick knew it.

Chapter 11

Kilo, Illy, Slugga, Babygurl, Keisha, and Cassy all sat in Slugga's trap, making money left and right. They had enough money and dope to let other niggas do the dirty work, but wanted to do it themselves. Babygurl had receive a text from the bartender and Babygurl told her to meet her at the trap. She was gon' put her on with her little movement she was putting together. She knew what the squad had going wouldn't last long and she wanted a back-up plan. Sale after sale came as she waited for ol' girl to come. She was finally giving up until a knock came and Illy answered it.

"Damn, gangsta, dope fiends getting badder by the day!" Illy yelled to Kilo. "What's up, what you need?"

"First off, I don't smoke no dope. Second, I'm not here for you. I'm here to see Babygurl."

Illy was about to get fly with her until Babygurl came up behind him.

"Illy, get yo' stupid ass out of the way. She came to see me. What's up, girl? Let's talk outside." When they got in front of the apartment, Babygurl noticed a gold Lexus on 24s with 5% tint. "That's you right there?"

"Yeah, that's me."

"I see you getting a li'l cash flow. What you do?" Babygurl asked.

"You know, I do a li'l bit of everything."

Babygurl shook her head and then reached in her bra to pull out a stack of cash. "You might not need it, but that's $5,000 dollars for looking out for us," she said handing her the stack.

"Shit, I need all I can get," she said while stuffing the money in her purse. "Look at me taking shit from you and I don't know your name. I'm Sadie."

"I'm Babygurl. Why did you help me that night?"

"I heard about y'all and I liked the way y'all roll," Sadie said.

Babygurl stepped back then looked her up and down and liked what she saw. Sadie was 5'9" and weighed 145 pounds with an ass and titties. Her pink muscle T-shirt exposed her six pack and her tight-fitting shorts showed off her sexy thighs. She had a golden skin color due to her being Black and Asian. Her slanted eyes and long straight hair made her look even more exotic.

"Since you like the way we roll, why don't you get down with what I got going on?" She explained to her everything from the squad to her little movement.

"Hell yeah, but my sister must ride with us. Trust me, we can be very useful," Sadie said.

"Cool, where she at?" Babygurl asked.

Sadie turned around and waved to her sister that had been sitting in the car. When her sister stepped out, Babygurl's eyes got big because she was identical to Sadie.

"Damn, y'all some bad-ass bitches," Babygurl said.

"This is Ladie. This is Babygurl."

Babygurl told Sadie and Ladie that they had to meet Keisha and Cassy first, then the squad. She texted Keisha and told them to come meet the new members. In no time, they came out and were introduced to each other. They were five bad bitches that could control anything. They chopped it up for a little bit, then made their way to meet Kilo, Illy, and Slugga. When the girls walked in, all eyes were on them. Kilo, Illy, and Slugga looked at each other with a confused look.

"Damn, Babygurl, what type of shit you got going on?" Slugga asked.

"This Sadie and Ladie. I'm sure y'all remember Sadie for helping us out at the club."

"I do, but what are they doin' here?" Kilo asked.

She hesitated before she said something. She knew Kilo knew something, but she waited on him to approach her about it. Before she could answer him, he called her to the back room.

"Tell me what you got goin' on before I got to figure this shit out myself," Kilo said.

"Those are my girls out there. In some kind of way they helped us out, and I wanted to buy their respect. I think we could use them on the team."

"What can they do for us?"

"I don't know, ask them? Look, talk to them and if you don't like what you hear, then I'll tell 'em to leave."

"Girl, I know what you got going on, and you better know what you doin. Call them in here."

"I learned from the best."

A couple of seconds, later Sadie and Ladie came in. Both of them were so fine that for the first few seconds, all Kilo could do was stare. "I appreciate y'all help at the club."

"It's cool. Real recognize real, ya feel me?" Sadie said.

He smiled because he liked what she said. "What type of shit y'all do to make money?"

"We do whateva, but we mainly set niggas and bitches up," Ladie said.

"We tryna get involved with what y'all got going on. If that's not too much to ask," said Sadie.

Kilo thought about what he was hearing and nodded his head in approval. He instantly came up with a plan which made him smile to himself. Neither Correy nor Quick knew anything about either one of them and he planned on putting them on them.

"I like what y'all got going on. Just make sure your loyalty lies with us and y'all will be good."

"That's what we vibe off of," Sadie said as they walked back up front.

Kilo had a plan that would put an end to Correy. He refused to let Correy get a piece of his city. He knew they wouldn't be able to resist a set of sexy-ass twins. Kilo had a smile on his face the whole time he was plotting against Correy.

***

Illy and Kilo had just finished dropping off some bricks in Kings Point apartments when Stronbone pulled them over. Kilo was in the passenger seat, so Stronbone walked to his side. He let the window down and lit a Newport.

"What's up, gangsta?" Stronbone said sarcastically.

Kilo hit his Newport and gave him a slight chuckle.

"Man, what the fuck do you want?" Illy said with hostility.

"I want to take y'all asses to jail for life, but I just can't seem to do it. I know y'all asses are the cause for all these killings and robberies, so tell me what y'all know."

"Come on now, you know how this is gon' play out," Kilo finally said, then passed the Newport to his brother.

"And how is that?"

"You asked the questions and we give you no answers, then you get mad and try to arrest us, but you can't," said Kilo as they both busted out laughing.

"You know I know about the little war you got going on with what's his name, Correy? I told him you was gon' come out on top, and from the bottom of my heart, I mean it. I only mean it so I can pin his body on your stupid ass," he said, making himself laugh hard.

What he said pissed Kilo off and his facial expression said it all. "Well, too bad, because it ain't no war goin' on. So step yo' detective skills up, gangsta," said Kilo.

"My detective skills can't be too bad if I know about that pretty baby mama of yours fucking with Quick."

Kilo's eyes got red at the sound of Lexi fucking with the enemy.

"Now if you don't mind, I got work to do. Please slip up so I can catch y'all black asses," he said, then walked off.

Kilo was so pissed off that he wasn't even paying attention to Illy.

Illy just pulled off without trying to get his attention anymore. He knew his brother's mind was made up on what he wanted to do to Lexi and he was gon' ride with him to the end.

Ray Vinci

Chapter 12

Correy and Quick were right behind Philly and Tidy as they made their way to meet the connect. They were scheduled to meet out of town, but the plans were changed, which made Correy more uncomfortable.

"So what's up, what do you think about this shit?" Correy asked Quick.

"Shit, this is what we need to take this bitch over!" Quick shot back.

"Whateva the outcome is, just be ready."

"Im just gon' have fun while I can, but before I go, I must get that bitch Keisha, or one of them niggas," Quick said.

Correy shook his head as he turned into a big-ass house that he could tell was decked out in the inside. They got out and met up with Philly and Tidy, then were escorted into the house by a beautiful Mexican girl. They were seated at a large table with food all over it. They sat there for a whole fifteen minutes before Escobar came and joined them. All of them ate before they started business. The whole time they ate, Escobar stared at Correy and Correy didn't know how to take it.

"So Philly, how long have we been doing business?" Escobar asked.

By him asking that question, he got everybody's attention.

"For a couple of years now. And it's been good," said Philly.

"Yes it has. Which is why I wanted to do better business. I want to give you more product for the same price," Escobar said, mainly looking at Correy.

Now Correy got his drift and agreed to what he was saying. He didn't know how he knew about him, but as of right now, he didn't care. What Correy was hearing made him smile from ear to ear. He was so into what Escobar was saying that he didn't notice Quick looking at him.

When everything was done, they stayed and partied with Escobar for the rest of the night. They were so drunk and high that Escobar let him and Quick stay in the pool house. He offered the same to Philly and Tidy, but they declined and went home.

They weren't in the pool house for thirty minutes when a soft knock hit the door.

Correy reached for his gun and answered the door. When he opened the door, two of the baddest Cuban bitches he'd ever seen walked in.

"Escobar told us to make sure y'all are comfortable. I'm Mary and this is my cousin Crystal," she said in broken English.

She was short and thick, which made Correy's dick jump through his jeans.

"I see that you're glad we came," she said as she dropped to her knees.

When she freed his dick, her eyes got big because she'd never seen anything so big and thick. "Oh papi!" she moaned as she played with it. "It's so huge."

She told him to sit down as she got between his legs and stuffed his dick in her mouth. They way she used her spit, he could tell she knew what she was doing, but he was too big for her to take. Whatever she couldn't put in her mouth, she jacked off while deep throating the rest.

"Damn, girl!" he said while letting her have her way with his dick.

She knew he was loving every minute of it so she sped up. When she knew he was about to nut, she looked up at him and he filled her mouth. She made sure she swallowed every bit of his nut. She waited for a minute to see if his dick would go down and was surprised when it didn't.

"You thought it was over? Naw, li'l mama, I just got started." He stood up and put her on her hands and knees.

He looked over at Quick, who was pounding Crystal from behind. She was small, so she was hollering from the dick game he was putting down. He tried to enter her fast, but was surprised by her tightness, so he slowed down.

"Yes, daddy! Yes! Oh, it's so fat," she moaned.

It was too much for her, but she still was gon' try and take it all. He was all the way in and still half of his dick was showing.

"Fuck me, fuck me with that dick!" she screamed as she tried to hack up on it. "I'm cumming, papi!"

He was slow stroking due to her being tight, but he sped up when she asked for it.

"Ahhhh fuck!"

"This is what you want, you betta take it all," Correy said while he stuffed Mary's fat ass. He was liking her because she was taking every inch he delivered. He flipped her on her back and for the first time, he saw how sexy she was. He put her feet in the air and slid in her with one long stroke. He could tell he hit her stomach because she backed up some.

"Ohhh! Fuck yeah, I'm coming on that dick!" she moaned, then started screaming in Spanish.

"Oh shit!" Correy said, then pulled out and came on her stomach.

She lay there as her body shook from the dick Correy had just put on her.

Correy lit a Sweet and all four of them got high and drunk to a new business deal.

***

Escobar was in his early 30s with the mind of a sixty-year-boss. He was Cuban and had been living in San Antonio with his father for twenty years now. Now that his pops was too old to run the family business, he passed it down to his son. He had been running the family business for three years and some change and had been watching the streets carefully. Kilo and Correy were of no interest to him until they started beefing and killing for his streets. He decided to put both teams on and see who came out on top. Both of them beefing was getting in the way of him making money and his father told him to do something about it.

He had just pulled up to his father's two story house when his father stepped out to meet him. He parked, then got out to greet his father.

"What's up, Papi, you doing okay?" Escobar asked.

"I'm good. Did you handle our little problem?"

"Yeah, I'm working on it now."

"What about Mr. Lee and Philly? Do they know anything about what's going on?"

"No, Papi, chill, I got things under control," Escobar said.

"I can't let these little punks mess up my streets. Every time I turn around, Kilo is robbing my spots and Correy is taking over my dope houses," he explained to his son with anger in his voice.

He knew his father and uncles had put everything they had to build the family and refused to let it all go to waste. Even though Mr. Lee was a dear friend to his father, he was with Kilo, so he had to go.

"If you can't handle it, let me know so I can make the call."

"I'll take care of it!"

He stormed off to his car. He was pissed off because his pops didn't believe he could handle it. His father's reach was unlimited and he knew it. He had started to come up with a plan that didn't involve him taking out Kilo and Correy. For the most part he liked them both, but Kilo had the streets on lock. When it came to the small things, Correy was a hustla by heart, so he decided to make as much money as he could while it lasted.

He drove off, then picked up his phone to make sure Correy got his dope and to make sure his money was in place. When he found out that everything was good, he calmed down. Kilo had been doing numbers with the work that he gave him and was wanting more and more. He had been keeping up on Kilo and his squad of killers and was liking their movement. He knew in time that they would be a problem and kept it in his mind to keep them close.

Ray Vinci

Chapter 13

Kilo had wanted to meet with Babygurl and her squad to let them know the plan. He and Illy had pulled up to the Elmira Hotel on Elmira Street and parked in front of the hotel room Babygurl had. He and Babygurl used to stay in this same room after every lick, which was why they knew there was a lot of money that way.

They got out and Kilo tapped the door once to let her know it was him. When the door opened, it was just Keisha, Sadie, and Ladie.

"What's up, Kilo, you good?" Keisha asked then let him in.

"Yeah, I'm good, where's Babygurl at?"

"Her and Cassy went to check up on some business."

He shook his head, then spoke to Sadie and Ladie. They were bad as hell and if the opportunity ever presented itself, he would tear the pussy up.

Kilo and Illy got comfortable as they waited for Babygurl and Cassy to come back. Keisha lit up a couple of Sweets, then passed them around.

"Y'all ain't got no drank in this bitch?" Illy asked Keisha.

"Naw, but I know y'all do," said Keisha.

Illy went to the car grabbed the bottle of codeine and Orange Crush soda that was in the backseat. He poured everybody up as they waited for Babygurl. Kilo was about to call Babygurl until they walked through the door with eyes big as saucers.

"What the hell is wrong with y'all?" Illy asked.

"Sadie and Ladie just put us on a lick that'll set us straight." She explained to them about what she saw and Kilo shook his head.

"That's for you and yo' girls, but if y'all need some help, let us know," Kilo said. "But anyways, I got a job for Sadie and Ladie."

They all looked at Kilo with a confused look on their faces.

"And what is that?" Babygurl asked.

"I want to put them on Correy and Quick. They don't know nothing about them, so it's the only way to get close to them without Correy knowing."

Babygurl smiled because it never surprised her that he was always on top of his game. She had already told them about their situation with Correy, but didn't tell them what she had planned.

Sadie and Ladie were eager to rise for the squad and show their loyalty.

"Shit its whateva, just give us the address," said Sadie.

He could tell Sadie was the leader of the two, so he talked to her.

"Alright, y'all ain't dealing with no anybody-ass niggas, so y'all have to play y'all's cards right. If y'all slip up one time, that's y'all ass. Sadie, I want you on Correy and Ladie on Quick. Wheneva y'all feel like the moment is right, let us know so we can off the niggas."

They all listened to him, making sure they got the plan including Illy.

When he was done, Babygurl pulled him to the side.

"What's up with it?" he asked while hitting the cup he had in his hand.

"What's wrong with you?"

"Nothing. I'm good. Just the more money, the more problems," he shot back.

"Nigga, you can miss me with that shit. I'm yo' ride or die. I know you."

He was gon' hold out, but he knew she wouldn't let it go. He explained everything that Detective Stronbone said about Lexi. While he was talking, he saw her getting more and more angry.

"Keisha, Cassy, let's take a ride real quick," she said, walking out of the door.

Keisha and Cassy grabbed their guns and left without saying a word.

Kilo knew where they were going and hoped everything added up in their favor.

***

Correy and Quick pulled in the parking spot in front of their apartment and waited a while before they got out. Since the beef with Kilo, neither one wanted to get caught slipping, so they stayed with each other. They stepped inside and were greeted by Lexi, Lovey, and Lisa.

"What's up, Lexi?" he asked while hugging her.

"Nothing. I'm good," she said.

Before anybody else could speak, Lexi's phone rang. She looked at the caller ID and was surprised when she saw Kilo's name and number pop up. She didn't want to answer it, but she did it anyway.

"Hello?" she said.

"That's how we doin' it now, half-breed?" he asked her, trying to stay calm.

"What are you talking about, Kilo?" She knew exactly what he was talking about, but she played dumb.

"You had to know I was gon' find out about you and that nigga."

"It ain't even like that. He was just taking me to get something to eat," she tried to explain.

"It don't even matter what you say. You chose yo' side. Just make sure you watch where you get seen with the nigga, because I don't care who he with," he said and then hung up.

Lexi was pissed off because Kilo had just threatened her like she was a nigga on the streets. Part of her couldn't be mad because she got caught red-handed with Quick. She forgot everybody was around until Quick said something.

"You good, li'l mama?"

"Yeah, I'm good," she said, not looking up.

"What that nigga tell you?" Lisa asked.

"He mad because I went out with Quick and he told me don't get caught slippin' with him."

"Bitch, I told yo' ass not to chill with that nigga. You know that nigga is crazy," Lisa said.

"Fuck that nigga! You good with me wherever we go," Quick said with confidence.

They chilled for a little while and smoked some doe-doe until Lexi calmed down. They all got up and walked outside to see Correy and Quick get in the car. Before they got in the car, bullets were flying their way. Correy and Quick instantly fell to the ground to get out of the way of the gunfire. The bullets that were coming ripped hole after hole in Correy's Yukon truck. Correy peeked at where the noise was coming from and saw who he wanted from the jump.

"It's them bitches!" Correy yelled to Quick.

He already knew who he was talking about and pulled out his gun. Correy knew she was over here because of Lexi, but this bitch had to die today. Without the bullets stopping, they still both jumped up blasting at them. Correy never let his finger off the trigga and ran out of bullets. Cassy came running their way with her gun busting at Quick so Keisha and Babygurl could come out. They all moved like they had been riding with each other for a long time. Correy stayed down because he knew not to expose himself. He knew Babygurl was a female version of Kilo.

When he realized that the bullet wasn't meant for him or Correy, he looked at the apartment. Lovey, Lexi, and Lisa were already inside but the door was still open. He saw Babygurl and Keisha moving towards the apartments. The outside wall had bullet holes up and down it, which made it look like Swiss cheese.

He tried to take off towards the door, but was stopped by Cassy sending bullets his way.

All at once, everything got quiet due to everybody running out of bullets. Correy and Quick jumped up and ran to the door. Babygurl, Keisha, and Cassy made their way back to their car. Before they drove off Correy, Quick, and Lexi came out.

Babygurl rolled down her window. "You chose the wrong side, bitch!" Babygurl yelled.

Lexi felt every word she said and knew Babygurl wouldn't stop until she was dead.

Ray Vinci

Chapter 14

Sadie and Ladie had been scoping out Correy and Quick for a couple of days now and were ready to pull up on them. They knew that Correy and Quick wouldn't be able to resist them, so it would be easy. They had put on some of their best shit and were now waiting on them to pull up at Skyline's hood store. Sadie knew that Correy always stopped at this store either before he went to check the trap or after.

"Were the fuck are these niggas at?" Ladie asked, getting impatient.

"They should be coming."

Right when she said that, Correy's grey Tahoe hit the corner and turned into the store. On cue, they both stepped out at the same time as Correy and Quick did. They both had to admit Correy and Quick were fine and had a swag that would make a bitch go crazy. Sadie made sure they got in front of them so they could check out their asses.

"Damn, li'l mama, slow down before you leave me and I won't get my chance to know you," Correy said to Sadie.

She turned around along with Ladie and it surprised Correy and Quick that they were twins.

"Boy, you wouldn't know what to do with all this anyway," Sadie said.

"All you gotta do is try me. I promise you'll find out different," he shot back, quick on his toes.

"And what about ya boy over here?" Ladie asked Correy, but looking at Quick.

"I'm pretty good at holding my own when it comes to something as fine as you," said Quick.

"Well if that's the case, I'm Ladie."

"I'm Quick."

Everybody exchanged info and went inside the store. Correy and Quick came out before them so when Sadie and Ladie came out, it was a surprise that they were still there.

"Shit, how about y'all come kick it with us for a li'l while?" Correy said to them both.

Sadie had her mind made up, but wanted to see what was on his.

"And how do I know you won't kidnap me?"

"I'm a hustla, not a kidnapper, plus you way too bad to be a kid," he said, joking. He made her smile and he knew he had her.

"Cool, I'll follow you," she said while they hopped in their Lexus.

Correy pulled off and Sadie jumped right behind him. She picked up her phone and dialed Kilo's number, which was answered on the third ring.

"What's up, Sadie, you good?"

"I'm betta than good. We on our way to chill with ya boy in Skyline."

"That's what I'm talking about. Make sure y'all careful. I'ma send somebody y'all's way just in case."

"Naw, we got this under control."

"Alright."

"And you owe us big time."

"I got y'all. Just make sure y'all good."

They were just pulling up to the trap when she hung up the phone. Sadie and Ladie laid down the plan one more time before they headed in the trap.

Little did Correy and Quick know they were gon' be chilling with the enemy.

***

The Sutton Homes were jumping and Slugga was getting every cent that came through. The Sutton Homes was low-key, under the radar, so nobody else was getting money but him. The day had just started and he had already made a nice bank roll. Dopefiend after dopefiend came and copped. Even dope dealers from everywhere on the eastside were copping. He was busy serving his clientele when his phone rang. He picked up quickly because of the traffic.

"What's up? Talk to me quick," he said, not caring who was on the other end.

"Hey, this Keisha. I need a favor."

He was surprised by the call because he wanted to get at Keisha, but never got the chance. "And what might that be?"

"It's slow and I need to make some money. Can a bitch come post up?"

"I ain't tripping. This bitch rolling hard as fuck," he said.

"Okay, I'm right around the corner," she said and then hung up.

He was already chilling on the porch, so he decided to wait there until she showed up. It didn't take her long to hit the block and when he saw her white Mercedes, he also saw a car that he had never seen before. The windows were tinted so he couldn't see inside. They kept driving as Keisha got out and he gave her a gun signal to remind her to grab her gun. She was looking good in her shorts and muscle T-shirt. Her red skin, fat ass, and big titties set her apart from every female in the apartments.

"I appreciate you for letting me post up at ya spot," she said as she sat next to him.

"It's all good. If I eat, you eat. Where ya homegirls at?" he asked.

"They went to some parties. I needed to make some money so I stayed back."

A sale came through and he told her to take it. She served him and before the dopefiend could leave, the same car that had come in behind Keisha had parked right next to her car.

"That's the same whip that followed you," he told Keisha. "I know that's some of Correy's niggas."

"It's only four of them. I know we can take 'em."

"Alright, let's see what these niggas talkin about."

He stood up and threw his hands up to see what they wanted. All four doors opened and the stepped out with guns. Keisha knew who they were because she used to fuck with Quick. She didn't say anything as she pulled her .350 semi-automatic out and started busting. The niggas ducked behind the doors, and Slugga took advantage of the situation and took off their way. Keisha was right behind him every step of the way. One of the niggas in the back seat raised up and shot their way, which made Slugga hide behind a building. As soon as he did it he came back out busting his .357 putting big holes in the hood of the car. Keisha let off the last few shots she had, which made the nigga jump in the car and leave. Slugga went to make sure Keisha was good then went inside.

"Shit, that might have slowed the money down for the day," he said.

"I ain't trippin'. I might as well kick it with you just in case they come back."

She reached in her purse and pulled out a bag of Kush then rolled up four Sweets. She lit one as Slugga turned on the NBA game that was in the PS4 already.

"I bet I can whoop yo' ass," said Keisha.

That caught him off-guard because he didn't know she played. "That's a bet."

They played and to his surprise, she was good. She beat him twice.

"I won, so I want my bet."

"We didn't bet shit."

"Shit, just give me some head and we'll call it even," she said, just playing.

He laughed and was about to say something back, but there was a knock at the door. It was a sale, so he made it and came back. Keisha was sitting on the couch on the phone when he decided to take her up on her offer. Without telling her anything, he dropped to his knees and reached for her shorts. They were Spandex shorts so they would be easy to get off. She didn't move as he tried to pull them off.

"I lost, so I'm paying what I owe."

She was still on the phone as she raised up and let him pull her shorts down. She didn't have panties on so when he got them off, her red pussy was popped out. He dove in tongue first and went to work. He slurped on her pussy as she talked on the phone. The conversation was cut short because Slugga was eating her pussy like a pro.

"Damn! Sssss, fuck!" she moaned.

She grinded her pussy in his face. She was cumming in no time. He stood up and was gon' walk off until she reached for his dick.

"We ain't done." She pulled his basketball shorts down.

His dick popped out and stood at full attention. She loved the way his dick looked and she knew she couldn't fit it in her mouth, but was gon' try. She stuffed his dick in her mouth as far as she could and sucked on it. She bopped up and down as she relaxed her throat. She used as much spit as she could while sucking and jacking him off at the same time.

"Damn, I been missing out on head like that."

She didn't respond but made all kinds of gagging, slurping, and choking noises. He had to back up before he nutted in her mouth.

They both took their clothes off and were ready to let each other have it. She laid back on the couch, put her feet in the air, and spread her legs wide open, exposing her fat wet pussy.

"Come put that dick on me."

He long stroked her in one motion and hit the back of her pussy. She backed up and his dick came out.

"Don't run," he said as he re-entered her. He banged her pussy in as she steady tried to get away.

"Oh shit! I feel you in my stomach. Fuck me, yes!" she screamed as she came on his dick.

He pounded a few more strokes before he flipped her on her knees. She poked her ass up and put her face in the pillows as he went back to work.

"Fuck! Shit! Ahhhh! Make this pussy cum!"

"Damn, this pussy on point. I'ma make this pussy mines."

"I'm...cumming, baby..." she got out between thrusts.

She tried to match him, but it was too much for her. She was flat on her stomach now and if he wasn't all the way in her before, he was now. She felt every inch of him inside of her pussy and was loving every bit of it. Her pussy was so wet that every time he plumped you heard the wetness.

"I'm cumming!" he cried out.

She got back on her knees and started throwing all of it back as hard as she could. In one motion, she made him fall back, then she sat reverse cowgirl and bounced up and down. At the sight of her ass jiggling, he busted a big nut inside of her. She stayed sitting on his dick until it was soft, then got up.

"I need to lose to you more often."

"Not no more. This is my dick now."

They chilled with each other for the rest of the day and made money.

Now that he had a ride or die, shit would be different.

Chapter 15

Nobody would be at the apartment today but Quick and Lexi, so today he had decided to shoot his shot. He had come out of the room in just his boxers and saw Lexi lying on the couch with her daughter asleep in her crib. When she saw Quick she got up and he saw that she had on some sweatpants and a regular shirt.

"What's up, li'l mama, you good or what?" he asked her.

It had been a couple of days since Babygurl and her squad had been by to shoot up the apartment, but he could tell it was still bothering her.

"I'm cool." She made her way to the bathroom.

He sat down, turned on the TV, and then waited for her to come out. She had been in there for a minute but it was cool, because he needed to think about how he would approach her. When she came out he could tell she had been crying. She sat next to him and he scooted over to comfort her.

"Talk to me, li'l mama."

"I fucked up. I left him and I knew the type of shit he did," she said between sobs. "The police pulled me over and I was done with his shit."

"Don't trip, mama, I got you," he said, trying to comfort her.

"I was seen with his enemy. That's what I shouldn't have done. Word got back to him and he sent his little girlfriend to come kill me."

"He not gon' fuck with you if I got something to do with it," he said with hostility in his voice. The more she talked the more he got pissed off. He was starting to care for Lexi and hated to see her cry.

"Let me know what I gotta do."

"Just be around to protect me."

"Let me know where I can find him so I can stop him from fucking with you." Part of it was game and part of it was real.

"I can tell you where he stays, but that's it," she said back without thinking about what she had just done.

He said nothing as he kissed her. She fell into it as he put her on his lap. He had his hands up her shirt and was rubbing her titties. Her moans were letting him know she liked it. He pulled her shirt over her head and started sucking her titties. He only had on his boxers so she felt his dick getting harder by the second.

"Damn, boy, what the hell you packing down there?" she asked when she felt him fully hard.

"Why don't you see for yourself?"

She got off of him, then pulled his boxers down, and his dick came out. All she could think about was the stories Lovey would tell her and Lisa about.

"Damn, Quick!"

She jacked him off and he seemed to grow bigger. She wrapped her lips around it then tried to deep throat it. She did her best at sucking his dick, but she knew it wasn't pleasing him. She stood up and took off her sweats, which revealed she had on no panties. He stared at her because she looked just like Lovey, but finer. Her ass was fatter without her clothes and her pussy was soaking wet, so he had to taste it. He told her to stand over his face and pulled her down.

"Ahhh!" she screamed out as he ate her pussy.

He smacked, sucked, and tried to slurp her cum out. It didn't take long for her to cum and she started shaking on his face. Without saying anything, she got off his face and jumped straight on his dick. She could only sit on half of it as she twirled in circles.

"Shit! Umm, oh my God!" she moaned.

He put his mouth on her titties to suppress his grunts. Her pussy was good, but he didn't want her to know. She surprised him and sat all the way down on his dick. He pumped a little bit inside of her and she encouraged him.

"Fuck me, Quick! Fuck me. This what you want!"

He picked her up and slammed her back down with a little force.

"Damn! Yessss, give it to me, make me cum!"

He put her on her back without taking his dick out. He pushed her feet to the back of the couch and long stroked her with force. She wanted to run, but couldn't go nowhere, so she had to take every inch. She creamed all over his dick as it turned white. She tried to say something, but was getting pounded, which made her come again.

"I'm cumming," He said as he pulled out and busted on her stomach and titties.

When he was done, they layed down and he promised her to protect her. He said that and got what he wanted from her.

***

Escobar had just dropped a load of bricks off to Kilo himself and was now heading to drop some off to Correy. This was really his first time riding through the east side and he could tell why they were fighting for each other's spots. It took him no time to get to Correy's spot off of Hackberry, which looked like a mini scene out of *New Jack City*.

He pulled up to their house, which had a lot of movement. He blew the horn and Correy, followed by Quick, came out. Correy waved him in then they both turned around and went back in.

When Escobar got inside, he saw two of the baddest twins sitting at the table counting money. He checked out the rest of the trap and remembered when his pops had started off like this.

He sat down on one of the chairs and lit a cigarette. "I like the way y'all do business. The money is coming pretty quick."

"Yeah, thanks to the shit you giving us. With it, we can take this shit over," Correy said.

"I hear y'all got a little competition out here," Escobar said, seeing what he would say.

"Yeah, but it's nothing we can't handle."

Quick was looking at him along with the two twins because all three knew he was talking about Kilo. He was gon' push a little more, but he had already decided to continue to do business with Kilo. He chose Kilo because he was already a boss and had the squad to take over. He would put Kilo on Correy when he felt he made enough money off of him.

"I got a load for you in the car that followed me here."

"I got your money over there on the table. My girls are just recounting it to make sure it's all there."

He picked up his phone and instantly someone was on the other end. "Bring them in."

Within a minute, four Spanish girls came in with two duffle bags full of bricks.

"Ten in each bag like you asked for."

Quick and the twins bagged up the money in their own duffle bags, then let the girls take them back out. Sadie and Ladie texted Kilo to let them know that Correy and Quick had just copped eighty bricks. They knew that Kilo always had somebody watching them so they were never worried about nothing.

"That's love."

"Correy, let me holla at you outside for a while."

They walked outside to the front porch and waited for the few niggas that were posted up to leave.

"Talk to me, Joe," said Correy.

"I've been in this game for a long time and I know a few people."

"So what's that got to do with me?"

"The streets talk, and some say you're in over your head with who you got beef with," Escobar said just to see his reaction.

Correy eyes instantly got red and his heart sped up a couple of beats, but he hid his anger.

"We good on our end, so you don't got shit to worry about. He walked back inside.

Escobar left and went straight to his father's house to check in.

Ray Vinci

Chapter 16

Kilo and his whole squad were sitting in his old trap, including Sadie and Ladie.

"Thanks to Sadie and Ladie here, we just found out about Correy copping eighty bricks," said Kilo.

"But we don't need that shit. We good on our end," Mr. Lee said.

"I know, but in order to take over, we must take out Correy."

"So we about to ride down through Hackberry?" asked Illy.

"You damn right!" Kilo shot back.

"Nigga, you know that's a death trap!" Illy shot back.

"It ain't nothing we can't handle."

Everybody agreed and then started getting ready.

"What's up Kilo, you good?" Babygurl asked as she hugged him.

"I'm good, Babygurl, what's on ya mind?"

"Nothing, just glad to be back home."

She and Kilo had been back on point since Lexi had left and she was glad.

"You ridin' with me and Illy."

"Cool."

Keisha and Cassy rode with Slugga and Felony, while the twins rode with Low-Key and Mr. Lee.

Kilo was leading the line as they turned off of Ferris and made their way down Martin L. King. Since Hackberry was like going into hell, they had strapped up with damn near every weapon they had. It took them five minutes to get to East Houston Street, then no time to hit Hackberry. Kilo knew Correy and Quick wouldn't be there, but they would pop every nigga inside.

They had pulled inside of the BBQ spot that was closed and walked the rest of the way. Illy was on the side of him when they made it to Correy's trap. Kilo looked at his watch and saw that it was 1:00 a.m., and the trap was jumping.

Low-Key spotted a blue Roadmaster in front of the trap making sale after sale. Without saying anything, he let his 40 cal loose on the car. It seemed like when the 40 started talking, everything else got quiet. The squad let their canons sound off along with Correy's goons. They knew it wouldn't be easy going to Hackberry and that's why Kilo made sure everybody stayed close. Kilo was next to Babygurl as bullets flew past their heads.

One almost hit Babygurl and Kilo knew one of them was close. He pushed her behind a car and spotted a nigga heading their way blasting shot after shot. Kilo was quick on his trigga and dropped him and he fell straight on his face. Kilo's attention was on the trap until he heard someone in his squad scream out.

He looked around and saw that Mr. Lee had been shot. Before he could help him, Mr. Lee's head was popped open. One of his squad members was dead, and it pissed him off.

The squad was smoking niggas left and right as they made their way to the trap house. Niggas were coming out of nowhere and the squad was running out of bullets. Everything was clear outside, but once they were in the trap, they had to pop a few niggas off.

"I want everything that's valuable to them niggas," Kilo yelled out in anger.

Illy knew his brother was fucked up about Mr. Lee, and knew now that it was really time to get at Correy. Slugga let them know that he needed help with the bricks that was in the back. When Kilo got to the back, his eyes popped out of his head.

"Damn! This nigga got big work in this bitch," Illy said.

"I'm glad we hit this bitch. Grab everything and let's get out of here before the cops come," Kilo said as he looked around the room for duffle bags. He found the same bags that the bricks came in.

They packed up everything and Kilo was glad that Sadie and Ladie had put in good work. Kilo knew that he had caught Correy slipping and he knew it would hurt him to lose eighty bricks. They made their way back to their whips and peeled off towards M.L.K.

It took them no time to get back to the trap and split everything up.

"Look out! Look out! Look out!" Kilo yelled over everybody because they were hyped up about the lick.

He grabbed a Ciroc bottle and the squad followed suit.

"I want to give a toast to Sadie and Ladie," he said, but was cut off by everybody's cheers. "They put on, but work is only halfway done. I got something for y'all."

He pulled out two black boxes and handed them to Sadie and Ladie. When they opened them, they pulled out two squad chains that everybody else had and smiled.

"Now y'all official!"

He pulled out Mr. Lee's chain, then put it on right on top of his. Everybody was quiet as they thought about Mr. Lee.

"Fuck all this sad-ass shit, I'm tryna celebrate!" Illy said, breaking the silence.

"Let's ride to B.J's and buy that bitch out," Slugga said.

Everybody agreed and then made their way to their cars.

***

Bianca was riding shotgun with Kilo while Slugga and Valarie were in the back. Kilo wanted to spend some time with Bianca because lately he had been too worried about Correy.

Kilo was in a deep conversation with Bianca when he saw a blue CTS on 26" Blades. Slugga must have spotted the same thing, but said nothing as Kilo followed the car.

"Baby, what's wrong with you?" she asked because she noticed his mood change.

"Nothin'. I'm good."

They were in Bianca's BMW, so he raised the windows up so no one could see inside. The CTS pulled inside of the Wal-Mart on Austin Highway and he did the same. He didn't know if Quick was by himself and really didn't care. When he saw who got out of the passenger side, his blood pressure shot up.

"Slugga, take them to the Landings and I'll be there in a li'l bit," he said as he got out.

Slugga already knew what it was as he got out and got in the driver seat. He pulled off and Kilo made his way inside of the Wal-Mart. It took him a couple of minutes to spot Lexi and he walked straight to her. When she saw him, her eyes got big. Her heart raced because she was scared, but she was also happy to see him. She was at a loss for words because she saw the fire in his eyes.

"You look like you've seen a ghost," he said through clenched teeth.

"Look! Let me explain."

"Bitch! Explain! What!"

She jumped and stepped back a little as he stepped forward.

"You ride around with the enemy like I don't matter, and don't act like you ain't fuck the nigga because I see the shit in yo' face. Then you got my seed ridin' with this nigga!" he yelled.

"Nigga, you fucked up and kept getting me jammed up with the laws."

"Like it's gon' be any different with this nigga? But the laws should be the least of yo' worries. The only reason I won't fire his ass up is because my shorty in that bitch."

She felt every threat that came out of his mouth and was glad that she had brought Heaven with her.

"You tell that nigga he betta watch his back because you not gon' be able to save him," he said and then walked off. "And if you with him, I'ma smoke yo' ass too."

She leaned against one of the shelves and started crying her eyes out.

Kilo made his way out of Wal-Mart. He wanted to air Quick out, but he knew he couldn't. He took off, walking towards the Landings with his hand on his banga the whole time.

Ray Vinci

Chapter 17

Detective Stronbone drove through the neighborhood like he wasn't a stranger. In reality, he had never been to this side of town. He was so used to doing his dirty work on the east side that he never came to this side of town. He pulled inside of a gym parking lot backwards so he could watch all movement coming or going. He thought about it and realized just how far along Kilo had come, from the slums to the suburbs. Kilo was making more money, driving better cars, and living in a bigger house that him and he wasn't even twenty-one years old yet.

As he thought about it, it pissed him off. It made him want to bring him down, or even kill him if he ever got the chance. Stronbone knew that he was beginning to be obsessed with bringing Kilo down, but he didn't give a damn. He had started ignoring his family just to spend extra time with this case. Stronbone had dirt on Kilo's squad and Correy's little operation, but didn't have enough to bring them down.

He leaned back in his seat to relax but was startled by his phone. He looked at the phone and instantly got frustrated.

"Hey honey everything okay?" he said calmly.

"You didn't come home last night, so I was worried."

"I'm sorry, I'm just real busy with this case. It seems like dead bodies are just popping up everywhere."

"Well, you must've forgot that we had plans last night," she said to remind him about the dinner date they had planned.

He had forgotten about that and it hurt him to where he had to wait before he spoke.

"I'm sorry. I'll make it up to you, I promise," he said, trying to convince her.

He never got a response because all he heard was the dial tone.

"Fuck!" he yelled and banged his fists on the steering wheel.

He jerked his head up because there was finally movement at Kilo's house. "About gotdamn time," he whispered to himself.

The brown Suburban pulled up to the house and just sat there. He sat there waiting to see what would happen, and was shocked by his phone. He answered it without looking, trying not to miss anything.

"Hello."

"Stronbone, where the hell are you!"

He knew that it was the chief by the voice and straightened up.

"I'm following up on a lead," said Stronbone.

"Well, it's a massacre on Hackberry Street, so get your ass down there and find out what's going on."

"Give me twenty minutes. I'm on the other side of town."

"Make it ten," the chief said and then hung up.

Stronbone let the phone drop in his lap and was back focused on the Suburban. When he saw the doors open up and two young black men get out, he figured it was some of Kilo's homeboys. He didn't want to waste time if it wasn't Kilo, so he peeled off to the east side.

He didn't know that he just missed a big crack in the case, and finding out later on would piss him off.

***

They had been sitting in front of Kilo's house for fifteen minutes when they finally decided to go in. Quick had sent them to find out anything they could and survive by any means. They didn't know who was inside, but knew somebody was there. They loaded up got out and made their way towards the house.

They figured that they didn't need any masks because somebody, or them, was gon' die.

They never noticed the unmarked car that was parked down the street.

One of them knocked on the door in hopes that someone answered without a care. It was early in the morning and in the suburbs, so no one was expecting beef. When the door opened, they both put their heatas to Babygurl's head.

"Move and that pretty ass face won't be so sexy."

She was caught slipping by herself and was mad as fuck. "What the fuck y'all want?" she asked calmly.

"Who else is in this bitch?" one asked as he pushed her inside.

"I'm by myself because if I wasn't, you wouldn't be living right now."

"You funny as hell, li'l mama, but you ain't in the position to be talking that hot shit."

"Nigga, fuck y'all and them niggas that sent y'all."

The other one didn't like what she said and smacked her in the back of the head with his banga, knocking her out cold.

They found some rope and tape and tied her up.

"Call Quick and tell him to go to the warehouse."

He got on the phone ASAP and then told Quick to meet him at the warehouse. Quick wanted to know what they had, but they told him it was a surprise. They carried her to the back of the Suburban and then threw her in. They peeled off like they had done nothing wrong.

The ride to the warehouse was quiet as they floated a Sweet back and forth. Since the warehouse was on the west side it took them awhile to get there. They instantly spotted Correy's Tahoe and Quick's CTS.

They parked in the back, pulled Babygurl out, and carried her in.

When Correy saw it was Babygurl, he got excited.

"Tie that bitch to a chair and I got the rest."

When she heard Correy's voice, she woke up.

"Rise and shine. It must hurt to wake up in hell," said Correy.

"And you gots to know that once Kilo finds out about this, you dead."

He laughed hard as they came back to tie her up in the chair.

"That's the last of my worries——" He was cut short by his phone ringing. "Hello! What? Ahhhh!" He threw his phone across the warehouse and backhanded Babygurl with all the strength in his body. Blood and spit flew out of her mouth as the whole chair flipped to the ground.

"Bitch, I know y'all had something do with my shit getting robbed, and we gon' be here all day until you tell me something."

Quick sat her back up while she was laughing.

"You know what's crazy? You already know we took yo' shit. It ain't nothing new to you," she said, laughing.

"You killed my mans, robbed me, and you think you gon' get away with it?" Correy said.

"Tell us where Kilo, Keisha, and the dope at, then we just might let you make it," said Quick.

She spit blood in his face for him disrespecting her like that. As soon as it landed on his face, he hit her with a right hook that sent her to the floor. He started kicking her in her stomach until she coughed up more blood.

"Bitch, I knew you was gon' be stubborn. I ought to blow yo fuckin brains out right now!" Quick said. He pulled out his gun and put it to her head.

"Naw, Joe, this is our way to get Kilo to come to us," Correy said while grabbing his arm.

"Today yo' lucky day," he told her and stormed off.

"Hey Quick!" he yelled back to him.

"Yeah."

"Call Lexi and tell her I said thanks, and I owe her one."

When Babygurl heard Lexi's name, she knew she was the one that gave them Kilo's address.

"You might as well tell that bitch that she dead once I get ahold of her," she said through swollen lips.

He said nothing as he took his heat and slapped her eye shut and instantly knocked her out.

Correy knew once Kilo found out about Babygurl, he would be mad and seek revenge.

Ray Vinci

Chapter 18

"Here you go, baby," Bianca said as she handed Kilo a glass of Ciroc.

"Thank you, li'l mama."

He sipped his cup and hit the blunt he had just lit. They had just finished counting up some money for his re-up. She was walking around in just her bra and panties and Kilo couldn't help but look at her fat ass.

"I still don't see how yo' ass so damn fat to be a white girl," he said while licking his lips.

She looked back and saw his dick was hard as hell.

"You love this fat ass?" she said walking towards him. She dropped straight to her knees and got between his legs. "I see you ain't the only one that likes this ass," She said when she pulled his dick out.

She put his dick in the back of her throat as she tried to suck the life out of him. She didn't need to come up for air, so she stayed down there using as much spit as she could. He sat there smoking his blunt, sipping his drank, and enjoyed getting his dick sucked. She made him feel like the boss he was and he loved her for making him feel like that. His phone rang which made him want to stop her, but he knew she wouldn't, so he answered it anyways.

"What's up, gangsta? Talk to me," he said through the phone.

"Nigga, is Babygurl with you?" Illy said through the phone.

"Naw, she at the crib. Why, what's up?"

"Because the girls went by to scoop her up and nobody answered. They checked the door and it was open, so they went in. When they got inside, Babygurl wasn't there," Illy explained.

"Nigga, what the fuck is you sayin'? Somebody broke in my shit and snatched her?" He yelled as he moved Bianca and got up.

"That's exactly what I'm saying. It's only what it looks like, gangsta."

"Everybody meet at the spot, and I mean every fuckin' body!" He hung up and then went to get dressed.

Bianca didn't say anything because she knew it had to be serious. As he left without say anything, she got prepared to do what he paid her to do.

Kilo jumped in his truck and peeled off. He had tried to call Babygurl, but her phone went straight to voicemail. He knew something had to be wrong, because she always picked up for him. Kilo made it to his spot on Skinnie's Block in no time and saw that the whole street was jam-packed.

He got out and walked straight inside. Everybody was quiet because they knew how he felt about Babygurl. He lit a Newport and let the smoke settle in.

"Somebody got my ride or die, which means somebody gots to die," Kilo said low, but it was so quiet that everybody still heard him. "I know who got her, but what I wanna know is, how did they know where the fuck she was?" Kilo spoke louder this time, letting them know he was mad.

"It's only a few people that knew where Kilo stayed, and I doubt any of my girls would sell her out," Keisha said, speaking up for her squad.

"If anybody in this squad gave up my shit and got my shorty snatched up, you betta pray that I don't find out," Kilo said. "I'm about to tear the streets up to find Babygurl, so y'all betta get ready."

He walked to the back and his immediate squad was right behind him.

"Don't worry, my nigga, we gon' find her," Felony said.

"I think I might know who gave up yo' spot," said Low-Key. "You might not believe it though."

"Who?"

"I wanna say Lexi. Besides us, she's the only one who knew where you stayed. Babygurl tried to air her out, plus she fucking that nigga Quick," Low-Key explained.

He nodded his head in agreement and lit up another Newport.

"We can find out where Babygurl is. You and Cassy need to go get that bitch Lexi," Sadie said to Keisha.

"When y'all find out where she is, let me know ASAP. Everything is shut down until we find Babygurl," Kilo said, then left.

Everybody went their own way as they set out to find Babygurl.

***

Word had gotten back to Escobar quickly about Kilo robbing Correy for the bricks that he had just dropped off. He also knew that Correy had responded by kidnapping Babygurl. Soon, Kilo would find out that the dope he got was coming from him. He thought about it for a minute and picked up his phone to call Correy.

"Correy, my friend, how's things on your end papi`?" Escobar asked.

"I'm good. Shit is hot right now, plus I got a lot on my plate," Correy said, not wanting to tell him about Kilo. So far, Kilo was winning their little war and he knew it.

Escobar's father had found out about Mr. Lee's death and told him to cut ties with Correy and Kilo.

"Correy, you know I can't do business with you while you're at war, right?" he said.

"So you saying our business is done?" Correy asked.

"Yeah, for now, papi."

"Nigga, I brought a lot of money to you and this is how you do me?"

"No hard feelings, but this is something I must do."

"Fuck you! Bad English speaking-ass nigga!"

Escobar never got the chance to say anything back because Correy had hung up. Next he dialed Kilo's number to let him know the same thing he told Correy. He knew this would be hard because he had actually liked Kilo. He didn't realize he was in a zone until he heard Kilo's voice.

"What's up, Kilo?"

"Escobar, you good my nigga?" Kilo asked.

"Yeah, but I need to talk to you about something.

"Okay, shoot."

"I'm hearing from the streets that you are going to war."

"Yeah, I am, but what's that got to do with you?"

"You know it's hard to do business while you got beef, right?"

Kilo understood where he was coming from and had already planned to shut down shop.

"Yeah, I feel what you talkin' about. As a matter of fact, I was just about to call you."

"About what?" Escobar asked him curiously.

"I know you was about to cut our business off, but I was gon' ask you, when everything is said and done, can we continue to make money."

He smiled because Kilo was a boss and understood the game better than Correy.

"Yeah, we can continue to do business, but what makes you think you will come out on top?" he asked.

"Because before I was a hustla, I was a killa. My homies will always come out on top."

Kilo hung up leaving Escobar there to think about his words. He liked the way Kilo moved and would most definitely do business with him when it was done. He knew what Kilo used to do and still did when it came down to it. People feared Kilo and his squad and Escobar could feel his gangsta aura whenever he was around. He continued to think about Kilo telling him about closing down shop until his little war was over. He couldn't put his finger on it until he thought about Correy.

He had just dropped them each off eighty bricks a piece, and Kilo had just jacked Correy for his eighty. Kilo was sitting on 160 bricks, maybe a little less, which would hold him down until shit was clear. He now understood why Correy was upset and Kilo was calm.

He saw Kilo as a thinker and knew that it wouldn't take his squad long to knock off Correy.

He picked up his phone and put it down. He was gon' call his father, but decided to wait until the outcome of the war.

Ray Vinci

Chapter 19

It had been two days that Babygurl was missing and her home-girls were starting to get impatient. Sadie and Ladie was on their way to meet Correy and Quick, and was hoping that they said anything about Babygurl. Sadie had pulled up to the Warren Inn apartments where they were supposed to meet up with Correy and Quick. The spot was jumping and evidently Kilo didn't know about it, because he would've been snatched it up. They stepped out of the Lexus, posted up on the hood, and waited.

All eyes were on them because they were the baddest bitches in the hood, plus nobody knew them. Everything was gravy until one of the hoes said something.

"Fuck y'all bitches want sittin' out here like y'all own this bitch?" one of the girls said.

"If we wanna own this bitch, we can, and it ain't shit you could do about it, bald head-ass bitch," Ladie said.

Ol' girl didn't like what Ladie said and pulled a switchblade out. "How about I cut all that long pretty hair off yo' Asian ass? Then we'll see who's bald-headed, bitch!"

Sadie and Ladie both pulled straps out of their purses at the sight of the blade.

"Go ahead if you wanna be laid up in a morgue," Sadie said.

Before anything could jump off, Correy and Quick hit the corner to stop whatever was about to go down.

"No need for all the drama. Shanta, go sit yo' ass down somewhere," said Correy.

They walked to their trap house that they had as Sadie plotted on how they were gon' get Babygurl. They walked inside and this bitch was decked out like a regular apartment.

"I thought this was a trap? This muthafucka looks more like y'all live here," Sadie said and Ladie nodded her head in agreement.

"It is a trap and it's a duck off," said Quick.

"I see y'all hold y'all's own when it comes to that gangsta shit," Correy said. "But what brings y'all to this side of town?"

"Shit, we just wanted to chill and make a li'l money," Sadie said.

"If that's cool with y'all," Ladie back-doored her sister.

"We ain't trippin'," Quick said.

Even if they wanted to tell them no, they couldn't because they were both bad as hell.

Ladie had got up and went to the car to grab some doe-doe, drank and handlebars. She knew once the handlebars kicked in, they would slip up. When she made it back in, they poured up. Correy and Quick popped two pills apiece and lit up Sweet after Sweet. It didn't take long for the bars to kick in, so they just waited.

"This for my nigga Rico." Correy said. then chugged his cup of Lean.

"We finally got that bitch," said Quick in a slur.

"What bitch?" Sadie asked.

"Because if she fuckin' with y'all, we can lay the bitch down," Ladie said, acting drunk.

"This bitch named Babygurl. We got her ass tied up in a warehouse on the west side. Her ass is as good as dead as soon as the rest of her crew comes to get her!" yelled Correy while falling on Sadie.

When they heard that they both tensed up. Sadie wanted to blow his head off right then but couldn't.

"Let us get that bitch." Ladie shot her shot again.

"You know what? I might let y'all do y'all's thing," said Correy.

They each took a deep breath of relief because soon they would know where Babygurl was.

They chilled as they made money and waited for the day until they were back with Babygurl.

***

Keisha and Cassy had been sitting in Spring Hill waiting to see Lexi so they could peel her wig back for telling. Cassy was about to say something until Keisha's phone rang.

"Hey baby, you alright?" she said to Slugga.

"Yeah, I'm good. Come to the spot. Sadie and Ladie got some info on Babygurl."

"Alright, we on our way. I love you."

She didn't have to tell Cassy shit because Felony had texted her while Keisha was on the phone.

She cranked up her Mercedes and started to pull off until she saw something out of the corner of her eye.

"There that bitch go right there!" Cassy said.

"Naw, that's her li'l sister Lisa, but she gon' have to do."

Keisha would settle for her due to her still trying to fuck with Slugga. She told Cassy to drive so she could handle up on Lisa.

"I'ma teach y'all to fuck with my girl," She said in a whisper as she crept up on Lisa. She had to move in a hurry because Lisa was almost to where she was going.

"Lisa!" she yelled as she got up on her.

"Your sister did this to you!" Keisha said as she put her banga to her forehead and put a quarter-sized hole in her head.

Everybody was screaming as Lisa flew off her feet and was dead before she hit the ground. Keisha was already in the passenger seat as Cassy drove out of Spring Hill calm.

"Stop real quick."

She jumped out and threw her gun in the drain, then got back in. She was glad that she did because as soon as they were about to get on the freeway, they got pulled over.

"Shit! Stay calm," Cassy said as she saw that it was the same cop that fucked with Felony.

"What's up, ladies? I'm surprised to see y'all without y'all li'l boyfriends," Detective Stronbone said.

"Why did you pull us over, Mr. Officer?" asked Cassy.

"I know all about y'all's homegirl going missing, and I know y'all about to get ready to paint the city red behind her. As a matter of fact, the day she got kidnapped I was there. But I blame y'all because if it wasn't for the killing y'all did on Hackberry, I would have caught who did it."

He could tell that they were getting mad at the thought of Babygurl getting snatched.

"We don't got nothin' to do with what you talkin' about. Since you a detective, shouldn't you be investigating my girl's case?" Keisha said.

"I frankly don't give a two fucks about her being kidnapped. I just want to put your whole squad in jail. I got enough information to give y'all each ten years apiece, but that ain't enough. Y'all ain't under arrest yet, but tell Kilo I'm coming for him." Detective Stronbone walked to his car as he got the call about the murder that Keisha just committed.

They took off quickly so they could get to the east side. Keisha was nervous as fuck because she had just smoked Lisa in front of the whole apartments. It was quiet the whole ride so it seemed like forever to get to Skinnie's block.

Cassy got out and Keisha stayed inside of the car and lit a blunt. Murder was on her mind and she needed her girl back. She was lost in her thoughts until Slugga got in the driver's seat.

"What's up, li'l mama?"

"I miss my girl and until we get her back, everybody that is associated with Lexi is dead," she said and then hit her blunt.

"I feel you. Just know that you ain't by yo'self."

"I know. Oh yeah, I just smoked her baby sister."

When she said that, Slugga's eyes got big, but he instantly said fuck it. They chose the wrong side and were gon' regret it.

They smoked the rest of the blunt together as he ran her down on Babygurl's situation. She was content with it and she told him about Detective Stronbone.

He came to the conclusion that Detective Stronbone knew too much, and he wanted to find out how.

Ray Vinci

Chapter 20

Everyone was sad about Lisa getting killed, especially Lexi and Lovey. They were both in the bedroom getting ready to go to Lisa's funeral when Correy came in.

"What's up, y'all ready?" he asked while sitting on the bed.

"Yeah," Lovey said.

He knew they were sad, but had to admit that they were strong. "Don't worry, Joe, I promise I got you."

She looked at him sideways and that's when she lost it.

"Y'all got my sister killed wit this stupid-ass shit y'all got going on! When you find them, you betta kill every last one of them." She cried on him for a while, then she pulled herself together and left.

They pulled up to the cemetery on New Braunfels in the Denver Heights. They were close to Pine Street so they felt safe from the main road. Since Lisa had been smoked, they had been nervous. They were beginning to take Kilo lightly until they took Babygurl, but now they knew he was serious. He decided that once the funeral was over, he would get Sadie and Ladie to off Babygurl.

The whole time the funeral was going on, they never noticed the two white vans that sat across the street. The funeral was well-protected by Killas just in case something went down. On instinct, Correy locked towards the van as the side doors slid open.

"Quick, they here!" Correy yelled as he pushed Lovey to the ground. Quick pushed Lexi down and reached for his heat.

The squad was already shooting up everything. Tombstones and grass were flying everywhere. Kilo and Illy started moving forward so they could get to Correy and Quick. Out of nowhere, somebody jumped from behind a tree and Illy chopped him in half with his AR-15. Niggas were dropping left and right on Correy's side, until Quick came from behind a tombstone and shot Low-Key in the face. Cassy was hit in the face with his brains and was almost caught off-guard. Felony was quick with his trigga and blasted on Quick, but missed.

Kilo was zeroed in on Lexi, who was hiding behind the casket with Lovey. If his Babygurl had to die, so would the bitch that gave her up.

He was cut off his path when he felt a burn in his left arm. He looked to where the shot came from and saw Correy. Kilo turned his attention to Correy and went crazy on his trigga. Correy ran for his life as he hid behind a tree. Kilo was already on his way towards Lexi and Lovey, who were still sitting in the same spot. He was standing over them and they didn't know until he said something.

"You snake-ass bitch! Tell Lisa I said what's up!" He pulled the trigga.

When he heard the gun click, it pissed him off. He was about to slap her with the gun, but he heard police sirens.

"Next time, Lovey gon' be buryin' yo' snake ass!"

"I'm sor——"

She was cut off by Kilos spit to her face. She looked up and he was gon' and instantly she knew her time would come.

They both stood up, looking for Correy and Quick, who were nowhere around. The whole funeral was messed up and bodies were everywhere. Lexi turned around and saw a face that messed her whole life up.

"Well, I see y'all life is just full of murder. You know, since y'all are the only ones left on the scene, I have to charge y'all with every murder here," he said, laughing.

They both stuck their hands out, ready to be arrested.

"Go ahead. We didn't do none of this anyways," said Lexi with her head down.

Detective Stronbone cuffed them as the rest of the people collected any evidence they could.

***

He was on his way to meet an old informant that owed him a favor or two. Personally he didn't like snitches, but he was gon' accept this one just to clear this case. Lexi and Lovey had been bailed out, but it didn't matter because neither one of them talked. He knew Kilo and Correy were behind the shootout, but he couldn't prove anything.

He pulled up to a park that was rarely used and spotted a black Lincoln town car sitting by itself. He knew who it was so he parked on the side of it and waited for the driver to get out. When the window rolled down, he knew he would be the one getting out.

"Get in the back," the driver said.

It pissed Stronbone off, but he let it slide. When he got in the back, he was expecting the father, but got the son.

"Where's the old man?" he asked.

"He's not feeling too good, so he sent me," Escobar said. "You might find out that I know more than you expect."

"And how is that?"

"I've been supplying your boys for a while now so I know everything they're up to. How do you think my father knows everything?"

"Well, where is Babygurl is? Because wherever she is, Kilo is going to make sure he gets her."

Stronbone had been on the Escobars' payroll for over fifteen years now and was eating pretty good.

"I know he has her in a warehouse on the west side where he goes every other day," Escobar said.

"When was the last time he's been there?" Stronbone asked.

"Today."

Stronbone got out of the car without saying anything. He was mad as shit due to Correy outsmarting him. He got on the phone quickly and dialed his old partner's number. It rang twice and was picked up by a female's voice.

"Grace, I need your help on something," he said as he peeled off.

"And what might that be?"

"I'm in a bit of a bind with this case, but I finally got a break. I need to know addresses for every abandoned warehouse on the west side."

"And what's in it for me?" she asked, even though she was already looking them up.

"You get credit for helping crack a big case, plus you get me in bed with nothing on," he said jokingly.

"I'll pass on the second one. Are you ready for the addresses?"

"Yeah, I'm ready."

She rattled off three addresses and he wrote them down.

"Thank you, you're a lifesaver," he said, then hung up.

He felt like he finally had Kilo where he wanted him. He had been wanting Kilo for years and now was his chance to get him.

He realized he was speeding for no reason and slowed down. He had all day and tomorrow before Correy would go back to the warehouse.

He got on the freeway and headed to the precinct so he could let the chief know what he'd just found out. It took him no time to get there, but he was stopped by the M.E.

"What's up, Stronbone? Let me talk to you real fast," the M.E. said.

"Okay, but make it quick."

"The bodies that were found in the graveyard, and the bodies found in Denver Heights, seems to have been done by the same people," she said, handing him her reports.

"I see," he said, checking them out.

"And the bullets on the graveyard bodies...some of them have your boys' fingerprints on them."

She never got a response as Stronbone took off towards the Chiefs office. He stormed right in just as the chief hung up the phone.

"What the hell is your problem?" the chief yelled.

Detective Stronbone told him about everything he had found out today.

"Okay, you got the search warrant for the warehouses and the backup. Don't make me look dumb for trusting you."

He walked out with the biggest smile on his face. He finally had Kilo and his squad by the nuts - not to mention Correy's crew.

Ray Vinci

Chapter 21

Kilo had been chilling at Keisha's and Babygurl's spot in Brackenridge apartments since he got shot. His left arm was bandaged up, but it still worked well. He had been laying low so he wouldn't put Bianca's life at risk as well.

Kilo was laid up on the couch smoking a blunt when Sadie came from the back room.

"What's up, Kilo, you good?" she asked as she sat on the other couch.

"Yeah, I'm just ready to get Babygurl back," he said, sitting up. He was just in his boxers, so Sadie finally got to see how fine he was.

"Let me and Ladie handle that. Just be ready to bust yo' guns on them niggas when the time comes." He passed her the blunt as Ladie came out in her bra and thong. She walked straight to the kitchen and Kilo watched as her ass jiggled. His dick got hard just looking at it.

"Alright, nigga, you betta watch out before Babygurl kill yo' ass," Sadie said as she noticed him looking at her sister's ass.

"I can look at whateva ass I wanna look at. I'm a grown-ass man." He stood up to grab the blunt and turned on the TV. Sadie noticed that he was primed up and said something.

"You need to put some clothes on before we call ya bluff."

"Who is we?" he asked, confused.

"Me and Ladie."

He laughed because he thought she was playing.

She took his laugh as a challenge and called Ladie.

"Ay yo, Ladie!"

"What's up, twin?" Ladie asked as she came in.

"Kilo got something he wants to show us."

"Oh yeah?" she said, waiting on what he had to show.

He didn't move, so Sadie went to where he was sitting and pulled his dick out.

"Well good morning to you too," Sadie said to his dick as it sprang out of his boxers.

Ladie came to join her as they both played with his dick. He contemplated on telling them no as they talked to each other in Japanese. He said fuck it and let them have their way. They both attacked his dick at the same time and kissed each other when they got to the same spot.

He was rock hard at the sight of these two bad-ass bitches going ham on his dick.

"Damn, girl, this dick here got some stamina," Ladie said, then deep throated him.

When she came up, Sadie went down. It had never taken them so long to make a nigga bust, so Kilo was a challenge. It took them fifteen minutes to get Kilo to nut and when he did, it was a lot.

"Oh shit!" Sadie said as his first load came.

He continued to cum as they both ate up everything that came up out of his dick.

"We gotta see if yo' dick game is good," said Ladie.

They both started getting naked but were stopped by bullets flying through the window. All three of them hit the floor as bullets flew everywhere. Sadie and Ladie crawled to the room and got their guns then came back to where Kilo was. Kilo reached for his twin Desert Eagles, and even though he was hurt, he was ready to ride.

The gunfire stopped, but Kilo knew it wasn't that easy and waited for them to come through the door. The front door was the only way in, so he waited.

"Get ready, because they coming!" he said to Sadie and Ladie.

As soon as he said that, the door was kicked in by a nigga with a 12 gauge shotgun. Kilo never gave him the chance and shot him twice in the chest. When he fell, two more came and Ladie molested her trigga until she dropped them both. All three of them got up as more kept coming, but they all kept dropping.

They were running out of bullets, so Kilo had to improvise.

"Hold them off!" he yelled over the gunfire.

He ran in the back and came back with a sawed-off Mossberg pump with a drum. He slid on the side of the door when he heard footsteps coming from the hallway. One came through the door, but was knocked out instantly as Kilo hit him in the face. He stood over him and shot him once in the head.

"Bitch-ass nigga," he said and started out of the door.

Sadie and Ladie were right behind him with their guns out. Nobody was outside and Kilo was glad because he was in pain. Sadie and Ladie just looked at him and at that moment they both fell in love with him. They loved the way he put it down, from hustling to banging his guns.

They packed up their shit and left before the laws came.

***

Bianca had picked Kilo up so she could take him to meet his squad. When he got in, he had a mini duffle bag full of money and set it in the backseat. She had told him she needed to tell him something when they were done with the meeting. She never pressured him to get out of the game, and he loved her for that. She even knew he was still fucking with Babygurl, but all she wanted was him.

"Look here, li'l mama. You see that bag back there?"

"Yeah, what about it?"

"If me or anybody you coming to meet needs to get out of jail, that's the money."

"How much is it?"

"1,000,000."

She said nothing as she pulled into Slugga's trap on the Northwest.

"I got another 2.8 million put up just in case you need it."

"Damn that's a lot of money. We gon' need it because I'm pregnant, Kilo."

He smiled at what she said and she did the same. Lexi was dead to him, so that meant his daughter was too.

"When it's all said and done, we gone. I got enough money for us to leave this alone."

They got out and then went to meet the squad.

Illy, Slugga, Felony, Keisha, Cassy, Sadie, and Ladie were waiting on him as they came in. It hurt him when he didn't see Mr. Lee, Low-Key, and Babygurl and he planned on getting revenge for them all.

"This is Bianca. She's very valuable to me in more ways than one. She's also our lawyer, just in case shit don't go right," explained Kilo.

"Kilo just gave me $1,000,000, but I'm pretty sure I'm gon' need more than that to make sure y'all get out."

"The money ain't a problem. However much you need, let us know," Felony said.

Once everything was situated on the lawyer thing, Kilo went straight to business.

"Okay, Sadie and Ladie, y'all up tomorrow. What y'all got in mind?"

"Shit, we ended up talkin' the nigga into letting us go air Babygurl out for them," Ladie said.

"And they fell for it?" Illy said.

"Hell yeah!" they said at the same time.

"Ain't no way in hell you can refuse us," Sadie said as they both posed. Kilo knew she was right, but kept it to himself.

"Y'all are some bad bitches," Bianca couldn't help but say.

"You ain't too bad yourself," Sadie said while looking her up and down.

"Anyways, what time are y'all gon' be at the warehouse?" Kilo asked.

"We don't know. We just know it's tomorrow, so just be ready for the text."

"When we get in there, somebody grab Babygurl and get out. After that, everything in that bitch that ain't with us gots to go," Slugga said.

They kicked it and talked about what they would do next, even though most of them thought there wouldn't be no next.

Ray Vinci

Chapter 22

He was pissed off to where it gave him a headache. He had the chance to smoke Kilo, but he had ran out of bullets. He had shot him in the arm before, so he felt like he had a shot at getting at him. Correy had sent some niggas his way thinking it would work, but Kilo smoked every last one of them. He smoked Sweet after Sweet trying to get rid of the headache, but it just wouldn't go away.

"Fuck!" he yelled and punched a hole in the wall.

Lovey and Lexi had left the same day the detective let them go, so it was just him and Quick there.

"Nigga, what the fuck is wrong with you?" Quick said, coming to the living room.

"How the fuck do we keep letting this bitch-ass nigga get away!"

"I don't know. He gots to have nine lives," Quick shot back.

"Well, if he got nine lives, then he must be on his ninth one."

"How about we go smoke that bitch of his?"

"We gon' let them hoes do it," said Correy while lighting another Sweet then hitting his bottle.

He felt like he had thought of everything and was fresh out of ideas. He should have listened to that damn detective when he said he was gon' lose. Being at war with Kilo caused him his connect, money, niggas, and Lovey. But Rico was like his brother and he refused to let a nigga or a bitch get away with his murder.

He passed the blunt to Quick because he knew he felt the same way.

"Tomorrow morning we finna go off that bitch."

"That's a bet, my nigga. That's a bet." He let the smoke settle in his lungs.

***

Detective Stronbone had been to every address that Grace gave him, and all of them turned out to be a dead end. The first thing that came to mind was to call Grace and chew her out, but he decided to make another call. It rang a couple of times then went to voicemail, so he hung up. He tried it again and Escobar answered.

"Detective Stronbone, talk to me."

"You fed me some phony information and I want to know why."

"I didn't give you no funny information."

"Yes, you did. I've been to damn near every abandoned warehouse on the got damn west side!" he yelled through the phone.

"You don't have no patience, Detective. You have to wait until tomorrow before anything happens."

Detective Stronbone was so anxious and ready to bust Kilo and Correy that he forgot he had one more day. He hadn't gotten any sleep in the last few days that he had lost track of time. He didn't even bother talking to Escobar anymore because he made him feel like he was going crazy. Detective Stronbone had pulled off from the last address on his list and started focusing on his next move. He was deep in thought when he spotted a car he knew too well.

"Well I'll be damned," he said out loud to himself.

He was a few cars behind it and wanted to follow it. He followed the car all the way to a warehouse that he would have never seen. When Correy jumped out by himself, it surprised him. He looked drunk and angry, so he knew he was going in to release some anger. To his surprise, Correy came back and forth with trash bags full of money.

"Oh, you just got you an all-purpose stash spot," he said out loud to himself.

He wanted to bust his ass right then and there, but decided to wait for tomorrow. Correy pulled off, but he stayed where he was. He would wait until shit got to jumping and be right in the mix of things.

***

She didn't know what time it was or how long she had been there, but she had a serious headache. She had heard somebody come in and out, which made her jump out of her sleep. She knew it was one of them coming to whoop her ass some more, but she was ready. They would come and try to get information about anything, but she would never give it up, so they would beat her ass. Her eyes was swollen, her lips felt like balloons, and it felt like her stomach was on fire. They would pistol whip her, stomp her, kick her, but they were never satisfied. She knew her squad was out there killing everything moving just to find her.

She was on the verge of giving up, thinking that her squad did. She had passed back out and prayed that her squad would be the next people she saw.

***

It was 2:00 a.m. and Kilo refused to go to sleep, as did the rest of the squad. Everybody was awake loading up every gun in the house. A million thoughts were running through Kilo's head, but only one mattered the most.

He lit a Newport and made a vow to himself that he was gon' kill Correy even if it killed him. He looked across the room and met his little brother's eyes. He knew those eyes too well and knew he had the same look in his eyes. They nodded their heads at each other, which was a nod of approval.

"Kilo, let me chop it up with you outside," Illy said.

Kilo got up and walked to his car and they both got inside. Illy lit up a blunt while Kilo put in Li'l Boosie's "Mind of a Maniac". They floated the blunt back and forth then finished it before they spoke.

"You good or what, nigga?" Illy asked.

"I'm straight."

"Whateva the outcome is, nigga, just know we had a good run." All he could do was laugh because he was right.

"Yeah, we built a nice li'l empire. I stacked a lot of cash while we was at it," Kilo said.

"I did too."

They sat in the car for about an hour and then headed back inside to kick it with the crew. When they walked in, the apartment was quiet as fuck.

"Y'all act like we about to go in this muthafucka and die or something," Illy said.

Everybody looked up at Illy and started laughing.

"Nigga, we know the squad don't fall to nobody," said Felony.

"R.I.P. to our fallen. We promise to ball out for y'all, my niggas," Kilo said before Slugga pulled him to the side.

"I know we always come out on top, but tonight something just don't feel right," said Slugga.

"I know, my nigga, I got that same feeling, but I gotta stay strong for my squad. I tell you what. Listen up, everybody. Keisha, Cassy, Sadie, and Ladie, once we get in there, I want y'all to grab Babygurl and get out."

"Hell naw, we riding to the end," said Sadie.

"What the fuck type of shit you on?" asked Keisha.

"Shit might not go right, so we want to make sure y'all good," said Slugga.

They were gon' argue some more, but saw that Kilo wasn't up for arguing. They stayed up for the rest of the night partying until Sadie got a call from Correy.

Ray Vinci

Chapter 23

Sadie and Ladie pulled inside of Spring Hill with Babygurl on their mind. She had started to think that Correy changed his mind because he waited so long to call. They weren't feeling the way Kilo had planned things out, but they knew not to argue with him.

When they pulled up, Quick was standing in the doorway with his shirt off.

"Bitch, I wish his fine ass wasn't the enemy," Ladie said.

"Me too."

They both checked their bangas, then got out to meet Correy and Quick. Neither one of them put their banga up, so Quick had no choice but to see 'em.

"Y'all act like y'all ready to ride down on us," Quick said.

"Naw, we just ready to ride for ours," Ladie said, making sure he understood what she was getting at.

"I like the way y'all roll."

He moved to the side and let them step inside. Correy was sitting on the couch blowing a Sweet when they stepped in.

"What's up, Sadie?" Correy asked.

"Hey daddy, you okay?" she asked, sitting next to him.

"Yeah, I'm good. Let's get this shit over with." He got up and both of them went to get ready.

"Shit, I'm glad we ain't wait all day for them to want to do this shit. Text Kilo and tell him to be ready," Ladie said.

She texted Kilo and told him to get ready. When she didn't get a text back, she knew he was running it to the squad. Kilo was on the other side of Spring Hill waiting on them to leave.

Correy came out and a couple of minutes later, Quick came out. They were both dressed like they were going out instead of putting in work.

"When we get in there, I'ma give that bitch one more chance to give up Kilo, and if she don't, smoke her ass," Correy said, then walked out of the door.

Correy and Quick got in the same car, but Sadie and Ladie went to theirs. They followed Correy out of the apartments and looked in their rearview mirror and saw Kilo. They knew the squad was right behind him, so they had no worries as they headed to the west side.

Correy was speeding, so it didn't take long to get there. The warehouse was tucked back, so Kilo circled the block to scope the place out. Once Sadie and Ladie met up with Correy and Quick, they made their way in the warehouse.

Even though it was sunny outside, the warehouse was cold and wet. They immediately spotted Babygurl sitting in a chair in the middle of the warehouse. When Sadie saw the way she looked, she wanted to shoot Correy right in the head. He walked straight to her and slapped her with all his might. She fell over, but Quick picked her up. Ladie pulled her heat and was ready to blast on Correy for hitting Babygurl.

When Babygurl noticed her girls, her eyes got big as she started crying.

"Bitch, this yo' last chance to give up that pussy-ass nigga," Correy said while kneeling in front of her.

"Fuck you! You dead and don't even know it," she said, laughing, which made him smirk.

"All you had to do was give that nigga up. I give it to you. You's a loyal muthafucka, but now you gots to die," Correy said.

"Naw, bitch-ass nigga you's about to die," Sadie said as she put her gun to his head. Ladie was on point as she aimed hers at Quick's.

"I knew something was off about y'all," said Correy.

They heard the back door to the warehouse open and saw Kilo and his squad come in.

"Niggas could never resist pussy," Kilo said with his gun trained on Correy.

Keisha and Cassy untied Babygurl and headed back outside.

"Alright, Sadie and Ladie, burn off," Slugga said.

They hesitated, then started walking off.

"Oh yeah, pussy, this is for Babygurl," Sadie said and shot Correy in the leg.

"Ahhhh!" he screamed as he fell to the floor.

Felony slapped Quick with his .45 and was right on top of him, beating his ass.

"Caught yo' bitch ass slippin'. You fuck with mines, you must die."

***

Detective Stronbone was outside briefing his team about the people that was in the warehouse. He was almost done when he heard the gunshot. The shot was loud due to the warehouse being empty. They were already suited up when the shot went off, so they took off running. When they got to the warehouse door, they slowed down.

"These boys are dangerous, so if you feel threatened, shoot," Detective Stronbone said.

He counted to three and they busted through the door with their M-16s drawn.

"Freeze! Nobody move! Drop your weapons and get on the ground!" Detective Stronbone yelled out.

Kilo pointed his gun at Stronbone and was about to shoot. The other officers were about to gun Kilo down until Stronbone said something.

"Don't shoot, fellas. I got this one."

"Nigga, if they don't shoot, I might shoot yo' stupid ass," Kilo said.

"You not that stupid to shoot me."

Detective Stronbone was walking up on Kilo cautiously because he knew Kilo was capable of shooting him. The whole time everybody's attention was on the cops so nobody saw Quick sneaking off. Kilo didn't give a fuck. He knew he was going to jail.

"Just give up, Kilo."

"Fuck you, pig-ass muthafucka!" Kilo yelled.

Stronbone had talked his way up on Kilo and tackled him to the ground. At the sight of that, Kilo's squad started shooting at the laws. Slugga was ducked behind a pillar as it was lit up by M-16 bullets. Felony let loose on a group and dropped two of them with no problem.

Illy was trained in on Correy as he tried to limp his way out of the warehouse. Illy damn near emptied his clip trying to get Correy. He almost had him until he was shot in the leg and then an officer was on him, putting handcuffs on him. Correy was next as an officer put handcuffs on him as well. Kilo watched one by one as his squad went down.

They had dragged all of them out to the curb in front of the warehouse and read them their rights.

"I finally got y'all black asses," Detective Stronbone said. "Y'all going to jail forever once I'm done with y'all."

"Fuck you," Kilo said

"One thing though. Two of y'all are dead, four of y'all are here, but I'm still missing five. Where are those pretty li'l hot mamas at? We know y'all came here to get Babygurl and she's nowhere to be found. Where she at?"

"Eat my dick."

"Right on."

They were all packed in the paddy wagons and hauled off to the county jail.

Chapter 24

"Kelvin Johnson. You got a visit!" The C.O. yelled as Kilo's cell door rolled open.

Kilo had been in jail for two weeks and with the charges he had pending, he knew he would be there for a long time. When he got to the visiting area, Babygurl was already sitting there. She was healing up from the beatings that Correy and Quick put on her. She was still sexy as hell, and she still held the title of his ride or die.

"What's up, my gangsta bitch?"

"You look like shit in that orange suit," she said, smiling.

"How you doing out there?"

"I'm good. Still trying to hold the streets down."

"I might be able to help you with that."

"And how you gon' do that in jail?" she asked, confused.

"You know, when you was out of commission, the squad hit the lottery."

She was still confused until she remembered when Correy kept asking her about his dope.

"How much?"

"Eighty, plus what we already had."

She smiled from ear to ear when she heard him say that. With that, she would be able to hold down the streets until she found another connect.

"You remember where we first stayed at when we got together?" he asked her.

"Yeah."

"Go check it out, and I need you to see if our boy is still holdin up on his end."

She already knew what he was talking about.

"Your attorney is here to visit you, so let me get to work."

He was glad that Babygurl was still holding the squad down. Now he saw why she was recruiting her team. He realized that there would never be an ending to Squad Up.

"Hey baby," Bianca said with tears in her eyes.

"What's up, li'l mama, why you crying? You knew the deal."

"I'm just happy to see you."

"Me too. Tell me something good, because I know you didn't travel this far with Babygurl for nothin'."

"I found a judge to take your case for what you gave me, but…"

"But what?" he asked, finishing her sentence.

"He can only do you for the money."

He put his head down to think of a plan.

"Give it to him and tell him to keep it a secret. Once I'm out, we can work on the squad."

"Okay, but you also have to leave the state once you get out."

***

Quick sat in the Motel 6 smoking a blunt and steadily looking out of the window.

"Boy, sit down with yo' scary ass. Them police ain't worried about you," Lexi said.

"What you need to be doin' is figuring out how you gon' get Correy up out of jail," Lovey said while snatching the Sweet from him.

"Don't worry about that. I'm workin on something."

He sat down and calmed his nerves. He wasn't just worried about the cops. He was worried about Babygurl. They had gotten away right before Stronbone ran in on them. He had barely gotten out of the warehouse alive and ran down a back alley. He had jumped a fence and to his surprise, he was helped by a man in his early forties. He introduced himself as Pablo and let him chill until shit died down. Pablo had told Quick to call him once he had the chance.

Little did Quick know that that was his come-up and he would still be at war with the squad over the streets of San Antonio.

To Be Continued...
Grimey Ways 3
Coming Soon

Lock Down Publications and Ca$h Presents assisted publishing packages.

BASIC PACKAGE $499
Editing
Cover Design
Formatting

UPGRADED PACKAGE $800
Typing
Editing
Cover Design
Formatting

ADVANCE PACKAGE $1,200
Typing
Editing
Cover Design
Formatting
Copyright registration
Proofreading
Upload book to Amazon

LDP SUPREME PACKAGE $1,500
Typing
Editing
Cover Design
Formatting
Copyright registration
Proofreading
Set up Amazon account
Upload book to Amazon

Advertise on LDP Amazon and Facebook page

***Other services available upon request. Additional charges may apply
Lock Down Publications
P.O. Box 944
Stockbridge, GA 30281-9998
Phone # 470 303-9761

Submission Guideline

Submit the first three chapters of your completed manuscript to ldpsubmissions@gmail.com, subject line: Your book's title. The manuscript must be in a .doc file and sent as an attachment. Document should be in Times New Roman, double spaced and in size 12 font. Also, provide your synopsis and full contact information. If sending multiple submissions, they must each be in a separate email.

Have a story but no way to send it electronically? You can still submit to LDP/Ca$h Presents. Send in the first three chapters, written or typed, of your completed manuscript to:

LDP: Submissions Dept
Po Box 944
Stockbridge, Ga 30281

DO NOT send original manuscript. Must be a duplicate.

Provide your synopsis and a cover letter containing your full contact information.

Thanks for considering LDP and Ca$h Presents.

<u>NEW RELEASES</u>

THE HEART OF A SAVAGE 4 by JIBRIL WILLIAMS
THE BIRTH OF A GANGSTER 2 by DELMONT PLAYER
LOYAL TO THE SOIL 3 by JIBRIL WILLIAMS
COKE BOYS by ROMELL TUKES
GRIMEY WAYS 2 by RAY VINCI

By **T.J. Edwards**

GORILLAZ IN THE BAY V

3X KRAZY III

STRAIGHT BEAST MODE III

De'Kari

KINGPIN KILLAZ IV

STREET KINGS III

PAID IN BLOOD III

CARTEL KILLAZ IV

DOPE GODS III

Hood Rich

SINS OF A HUSTLA II

ASAD

RICH $AVAGE II

By **Martell Troublesome Bolden**

YAYO V

Bred In The Game 2

S. Allen

CREAM III

THE STREETS WILL TALK II

By **Yolanda Moore**

SON OF A DOPE FIEND III

HEAVEN GOT A GHETTO II

By **Renta**

LOYALTY AIN'T PROMISED III

By **Keith Williams**

I'M NOTHING WITHOUT HIS LOVE II

SINS OF A THUG II

TO THE THUG I LOVED BEFORE II

IN A HUSTLER I TRUST II

By Monet Dragun

QUIET MONEY IV

EXTENDED CLIP III

THUG LIFE IV

By **Trai'Quan**

THE STREETS MADE ME IV

By **Larry D. Wright**

IF YOU CROSS ME ONCE II

ANGEL IV

By **Anthony Fields**

THE STREETS WILL NEVER CLOSE IV

By K'ajji

HARD AND RUTHLESS III

KILLA KOUNTY III

By Khufu

MONEY GAME III

By Smoove Dolla

JACK BOYS VS DOPE BOYS II

A GANGSTA'S QUR'AN V

COKE GIRLZ II

COKE BOYS II

By Romell Tukes

MURDA WAS THE CASE II

Elijah R. Freeman

THE STREETS NEVER LET GO II

By Robert Baptiste

AN UNFORESEEN LOVE III

By **Meesha**

KING OF THE TRENCHES III
by **GHOST & TRANAY ADAMS**

MONEY MAFIA II

By **Jibril Williams**

QUEEN OF THE ZOO III

By **Black Migo**

VICIOUS LOYALTY III

By Kingpen

A GANGSTA'S PAIN III

By J-Blunt

CONFESSIONS OF A JACKBOY III

By Nicholas Lock

GRIMEY WAYS III

By Ray Vinci

KING KILLA II

By Vincent "Vitto" Holloway

BETRAYAL OF A THUG II

By Fre$h

THE MURDER QUEENS II

By Michael Gallon

THE BIRTH OF A GANGSTER III

By Delmont Player

TREAL LOVE II

By Le'Monica Jackson

FOR THE LOVE OF BLOOD II

By Jamel Mitchell

RAN OFF ON DA PLUG II

By Paper Boi Rari

HOOD CONSIGLIERE II

By Keese

PRETTY GIRLS DO NASTY THINGS II

By Nicole Goosby

PROTÉGÉ OF A LEGEND II

By Corey Robinson

IT'S JUST ME AND YOU II

By Ah'Million

Available Now

RESTRAINING ORDER **I & II**

By **CA$H & Coffee**

LOVE KNOWS NO BOUNDARIES **I II & III**

By **Coffee**

RAISED AS A GOON I, II, III & IV

BRED BY THE SLUMS I, II, III

BLAST FOR ME I & II

ROTTEN TO THE CORE I II III

A BRONX TALE I, II, III

DUFFLE BAG CARTEL I II III IV V VI

HEARTLESS GOON I II III IV V

A SAVAGE DOPEBOY I II

DRUG LORDS I II III

CUTTHROAT MAFIA I II

KING OF THE TRENCHES

By **Ghost**

LAY IT DOWN **I & II**

LAST OF A DYING BREED I II

BLOOD STAINS OF A SHOTTA I & II III

By **Jamaica**

LOYAL TO THE GAME I II III

LIFE OF SIN I, II III

By **TJ & Jelissa**

BLOODY COMMAS I & II

SKI MASK CARTEL I II & III

KING OF NEW YORK I II,III IV V

RISE TO POWER I II III

COKE KINGS I II III IV V

BORN HEARTLESS I II III IV

KING OF THE TRAP I II

By **T.J. Edwards**

IF LOVING HIM IS WRONG…I & II

LOVE ME EVEN WHEN IT HURTS I II III

By **Jelissa**

WHEN THE STREETS CLAP BACK I & II III

Ray Vinci

THE HEART OF A SAVAGE I II III IV

MONEY MAFIA

LOYAL TO THE SOIL I II III

By **Jibril Williams**

A DISTINGUISHED THUG STOLE MY HEART I II & III

LOVE SHOULDN'T HURT I II III IV

RENEGADE BOYS I II III IV

PAID IN KARMA I II III

SAVAGE STORMS I II III

AN UNFORESEEN LOVE I II

By **Meesha**

A GANGSTER'S CODE I &, II III

A GANGSTER'S SYN I II III

THE SAVAGE LIFE I II III

CHAINED TO THE STREETS I II III

BLOOD ON THE MONEY I II III

A GANGSTA'S PAIN I II

By J-Blunt

PUSH IT TO THE LIMIT

By **Bre' Hayes**

BLOOD OF A BOSS **I, II, III, IV, V**

SHADOWS OF THE GAME

TRAP BASTARD

By **Askari**

THE STREETS BLEED MURDER **I, II & III**

THE HEART OF A GANGSTA I II& III

By **Jerry Jackson**

168

CUM FOR ME I II III IV V VI VII VIII

An **LDP Erotica Collaboration**

BRIDE OF A HUSTLA **I II & II**

THE FETTI GIRLS **I, II& III**

CORRUPTED BY A GANGSTA I, II III, IV

BLINDED BY HIS LOVE

THE PRICE YOU PAY FOR LOVE I, II ,III

DOPE GIRL MAGIC I II III

By **Destiny Skai**

WHEN A GOOD GIRL GOES BAD

By **Adrienne**

THE COST OF LOYALTY I II III

By Kweli

A GANGSTER'S REVENGE **I II III & IV**

THE BOSS MAN'S DAUGHTERS I II III IV V

A SAVAGE LOVE **I & II**

BAE BELONGS TO ME I II

A HUSTLER'S DECEIT I, II, III

WHAT BAD BITCHES DO I, II, III

SOUL OF A MONSTER I II III

KILL ZONE

A DOPE BOY'S QUEEN I II III

TIL DEATH

By **Aryanna**

A KINGPIN'S AMBITON

A KINGPIN'S AMBITION **II**

I MURDER FOR THE DOUGH

Ray Vinci

By **Ambitious**
TRUE SAVAGE I II III IV V VI VII
DOPE BOY MAGIC I, II, III
MIDNIGHT CARTEL I II III
CITY OF KINGZ I II
NIGHTMARE ON SILENT AVE
THE PLUG OF LIL MEXICO II
CLASSIC CITY
By **Chris Green**
A DOPEBOY'S PRAYER
By **Eddie "Wolf" Lee**
THE KING CARTEL **I, II & III**
By **Frank Gresham**
THESE NIGGAS AIN'T LOYAL **I, II & III**
By **Nikki Tee**
GANGSTA SHYT **I II &III**
By **CATO**
THE ULTIMATE BETRAYAL
By **Phoenix**
BOSS'N UP **I , II & III**
By **Royal Nicole**
I LOVE YOU TO DEATH
By **Destiny J**
I RIDE FOR MY HITTA
I STILL RIDE FOR MY HITTA
By **Misty Holt**
LOVE & CHASIN' PAPER

By **Qay Crockett**

TO DIE IN VAIN

SINS OF A HUSTLA

By **ASAD**

BROOKLYN HUSTLAZ

By **Boogsy Morina**

BROOKLYN ON LOCK I & II

By **Sonovia**

GANGSTA CITY

By **Teddy Duke**

A DRUG KING AND HIS DIAMOND I & II III

A DOPEMAN'S RICHES

HER MAN, MINE'S TOO I, II

CASH MONEY HO'S

THE WIFEY I USED TO BE I II

PRETTY GIRLS DO NASTY THINGS

By Nicole Goosby

TRAPHOUSE KING **I II & III**

KINGPIN KILLAZ I II III

STREET KINGS I II

PAID IN BLOOD **I II**

CARTEL KILLAZ I II III

DOPE GODS I II

By **Hood Rich**

LIPSTICK KILLAH **I, II, III**

CRIME OF PASSION I II & III

FRIEND OR FOE I II III

By **Mimi**

STEADY MOBBN' **I, II, III**

THE STREETS STAINED MY SOUL I II III

By **Marcellus Allen**

WHO SHOT YA **I, II, III**

SON OF A DOPE FIEND I II

HEAVEN GOT A GHETTO

Renta

GORILLAZ IN THE BAY **I II III IV**

TEARS OF A GANGSTA I II

3X KRAZY I II

STRAIGHT BEAST MODE I II

DE'KARI

TRIGGADALE I II III

MURDAROBER WAS THE CASE

Elijah R. Freeman

GOD BLESS THE TRAPPERS I, II, III

THESE SCANDALOUS STREETS I, II, III

FEAR MY GANGSTA I, II, III IV, V

THESE STREETS DON'T LOVE NOBODY I, II

BURY ME A G I, II, III, IV, V

A GANGSTA'S EMPIRE I, II, III, IV

THE DOPEMAN'S BODYGAURD I II

THE REALEST KILLAZ I II III

THE LAST OF THE OGS I II III

Tranay Adams

THE STREETS ARE CALLING

Duquie Wilson

MARRIED TO A BOSS I II III

By Destiny Skai & Chris Green

KINGZ OF THE GAME I II III IV V VI

Playa Ray

SLAUGHTER GANG I II III

RUTHLESS HEART I II III

By Willie Slaughter

FUK SHYT

By Blakk Diamond

DON'T F#CK WITH MY HEART I II

By Linnea

ADDICTED TO THE DRAMA I II III

IN THE ARM OF HIS BOSS II

By Jamila

YAYO I II III IV

A SHOOTER'S AMBITION I II

BRED IN THE GAME

By S. Allen

TRAP GOD I II III

RICH $AVAGE

MONEY IN THE GRAVE I II III

By Martell Troublesome Bolden

FOREVER GANGSTA

GLOCKS ON SATIN SHEETS I II

By Adrian Dulan

TOE TAGZ I II III IV

Ray Vinci

LEVELS TO THIS SHYT I II

IT'S JUST ME AND YOU

By Ah'Million

KINGPIN DREAMS I II III

RAN OFF ON DA PLUG

By Paper Boi Rari

CONFESSIONS OF A GANGSTA I II III IV

CONFESSIONS OF A JACKBOY I II

By Nicholas Lock

I'M NOTHING WITHOUT HIS LOVE

SINS OF A THUG

TO THE THUG I LOVED BEFORE

A GANGSTA SAVED XMAS

IN A HUSTLER I TRUST

By Monet Dragun

CAUGHT UP IN THE LIFE I II III

THE STREETS NEVER LET GO

By Robert Baptiste

NEW TO THE GAME I II III

MONEY, MURDER & MEMORIES I II III

By **Malik D. Rice**

LIFE OF A SAVAGE I II III

A GANGSTA'S QUR'AN I II III IV

MURDA SEASON I II III

GANGLAND CARTEL I II III

CHI'RAQ GANGSTAS I II III

KILLERS ON ELM STREET I II III

JACK BOYZ N DA BRONX I II III

A DOPEBOY'S DREAM I II III

JACK BOYS VS DOPE BOYS

COKE GIRLZ

COKE BOYS

By Romell Tukes

LOYALTY AIN'T PROMISED I II

By Keith Williams

QUIET MONEY I II III

THUG LIFE I II III

EXTENDED CLIP I II

By **Trai'Quan**

THE STREETS MADE ME I II III

By **Larry D. Wright**

THE ULTIMATE SACRIFICE I, II, III, IV, V, VI

KHADIFI

IF YOU CROSS ME ONCE

ANGEL I II III

IN THE BLINK OF AN EYE

By **Anthony Fields**

THE LIFE OF A HOOD STAR

By Ca$h & Rashia Wilson

THE STREETS WILL NEVER CLOSE I II III

By K'ajji

CREAM I II

THE STREETS WILL TALK

By Yolanda Moore

NIGHTMARES OF A HUSTLA I II III

By King Dream

CONCRETE KILLA I II III

VICIOUS LOYALTY I II

By Kingpen

HARD AND RUTHLESS I II

MOB TOWN 251

THE BILLIONAIRE BENTLEYS I II III

By Von Diesel

GHOST MOB

Stilloan Robinson

MOB TIES I II III IV V VI

By SayNoMore

BODYMORE MURDERLAND I II III

THE BIRTH OF A GANGSTER I II

By Delmont Player

FOR THE LOVE OF A BOSS

By C. D. Blue

MOBBED UP I II III IV

THE BRICK MAN I II III IV

THE COCAINE PRINCESS I II III IV V

By King Rio

KILLA KOUNTY I II III

By Khufu

MONEY GAME I II

By Smoove Dolla

A GANGSTA'S KARMA I II

By FLAME
KING OF THE TRENCHES I II
by **GHOST & TRANAY ADAMS**
QUEEN OF THE ZOO I II
By **Black Migo**
GRIMEY WAYS I II
By Ray Vinci
XMAS WITH AN ATL SHOOTER
By Ca$h & Destiny Skai
KING KILLA
By Vincent "Vitto" Holloway
BETRAYAL OF A THUG
By Fre$h
THE MURDER QUEENS
By Michael Gallon
TREAL LOVE
By Le'Monica Jackson
FOR THE LOVE OF BLOOD
By Jamel Mitchell
HOOD CONSIGLIERE
By Keese
PROTÉGÉ OF A LEGEND
By Corey Robinson

<u>BOOKS BY LDP'S CEO, CA$H</u>

TRUST IN NO MAN

TRUST IN NO MAN 2

TRUST IN NO MAN 3

BONDED BY BLOOD

SHORTY GOT A THUG

THUGS CRY

THUGS CRY 2

THUGS CRY 3

TRUST NO BITCH

TRUST NO BITCH 2

TRUST NO BITCH 3

TIL MY CASKET DROPS

RESTRAINING ORDER

RESTRAINING ORDER 2

IN LOVE WITH A CONVICT

LIFE OF A HOOD STAR

XMAS WITH AN ATL SHOOTER

Grimey Ways 2

CPSIA information can be obtained
at www.ICGtesting.com
Printed in the USA
LVHW011110110822
725708LV00008B/501